Empire
of the
Grotesque

EMPIRE OF THE GROTESQUE

TOM MALONE

"They attacked the plane on the ground?"

"Yes, sir."

"But our people managed to take off successfully?"

"There were some problems."

"Problems?"

"As the jet started to take off from the airport one of the Bolivian demonstrators got stuck on the wing. His foot got caught in the aileron somehow. When the diplomatic mission inside looked out and saw what was going on there was some concern."

The Section Chief frowned and removed his glasses. He looked annoyed. "I'm sure there was. And they did what?"

"Nothing. They couldn't abort their flight at that point. They were committed. It didn't turn out happily for the demonstrator."

"There was no word in the press for obvious reasons."

"According to some of our informants the pilot also ran over a couple of Bolivians taxiing to take off."

"Needleman was the Special Envoy on this mission?"

"Yes. And Mote was head of the security team."

The Section Chief replaced his glasses. "Mote again," he said under his breath, as if the words left a bad taste in his mouth. "That name seems to come up a lot. More than someone of his rank usually does."

L. nodded but didn't speak. Well, of course, that was Conrad Mote for you. A magnet for disaster. Always managing to get in the thick of things. Never in a lead role, of course, a key player, but always involved some-how. Always making his contribution to the further exac-erbation of any situation.

The desert would be as good a place as any to begin. He could see it starting off like some bad movie:

FADE IN: *An aerial view of a parched desert landscape shimmering in the heat. Sulfurous clouds drift beneath us; we hold for a second until:*

A streak of dust comes into frame, rocketing over the toxic salt flats. Even from this height it is apparent the vehicle is moving at tremendous speed. It is followed seconds later by other stretching fingers of dust. We angle down for a closer look now, past the spinning wheels and in through the win-dow of the lead pursuit vehicle.

"Come on you piece of crap!" Conrad Mote is shout-ing over the terrible racket, dust billowing up through the broken floorboards. Bob Durwood sits next to him, strapped down hard in his seat, choking, blinded by the smoke and dust, his face is a hive of twitches as they suddenly go airborne, soaring in a weightless, stomach-turning arc. They hit the desert floor with a spine-crunching jolt. Something comes loose in the suspension now, banging against the twisted frame. The whole machine seems ready to come apart. "Chinese piece of dog shit!" Mote hisses, fighting against the wheel. He is wearing heavy gloves, his red face covered with sweat.

Quattlebaum was just ahead, a spinning, twisting dust devil—close enough to catch the flash of his silver helmet.

Mote tries some fancy shifting now, torturing the gearbox again. He has an insane look on his face, eyes vicious little slits. "Improper social programming, my ass!" he says, bouncing up and down in his seat. He blasts the heart out of a huge saguaro cactus, punches the wipers to clear off the pulp and ooze and a few stray feathers from the windshield. He gives Durwood a venomous look. "Bastard thinks he's clever. Always *sooo* fucking clever! But let's see him get out of this one! We've got his slick ass now."

The radio suddenly erupts with excited voices. Everyone gibbering at once. Choppers confirm their arrival in a few minutes, converging from all points of the compass. The net was closing rapidly. The Great Quattlebaum was running out of moves, methodically being surrounded and run to ground.

Mote turns to Bob with a lopsided murderous grin.

"Heh, heh . . . Been waiting for this for a long time."

Bob was beginning to suspect the man was deranged. "What is it, something personal with you, Mote?"

"Damn right it's personal!" Mote shouts over the wall of noise. "Bastard switched hats on me in a restaurant! Gave me one loaded with explosives. When I went outside he detonated it with a cell phone . . ."

Quattlebaum suddenly veers hard left, heading out of the open areas towards the rocks. Mote cranks the wheel instinctively, narrowly missing a huge block of granite.

"Watch where you're driving," Bob croaks.

Mote grins, pays no attention, grazes another rock. "Luckily it was mostly a dud ... Not much of an explosion really. Busted both my eardrums though ... An old Marine LZ marker bomb that turned my hair day-glo green for a couple months ... Not good in my business... Not when you're security. Dizzy as hell for a long time too."

Now Bob knew where he had seen him before. He couldn't place him at first when they met at the briefing before the operation, but now he remembered. The green hair. The bandages. Then the flying bottles. He had seen him on the *World News*. Standing on some desolate, wind-blown runway in the Fourth-World, eyeing the crowd suspiciously for weapons as El Supremo's diplomats tried to give a speech.

"Where was it?"

"What?"

"Where you guys started the civil war."

Mote gave him a shifty look out of the corner of his

eye, seemed embarrassed. "Hey, look, it wasn't our fault really. It was totally fucked to begin with. I was just head of security, nothing else. The crowd was so drunk by the time we got there—our flight was three hours late—they didn't really know who we were. Thought we were some kind of fuckin' rock band. When they found out we didn't play instruments and were just government bureaucrats things got nasty."

• • •

"Let's begin again . . ."

The Section Chief spread his hands out on the papers and pursed his lips. The loose flesh on his face and meaty lips gave the expression a slightly comical look, totally at odds with the magisterial demeanor he was trying with little success to convey.

He cleared his throat and began speaking. "There are several points here that need to be examined." A slight pause now for emphasis. "We need to be rigorously thorough so there can be absolutely no questions later on. No uncertainties that would support second guessing upon subsequent review."

The other five men in the room seated at the long highly polished table of dark wood made no comment. They all wore blank expressions. They looked neither friendly nor unfriendly, interested or disinterested in the proceedings. They could have been mannequins. L., looking out of place, dressed in a olive drab, shapeless suit, was uncomfortable. He was trying to stay focused. Outside the bullet proof windows an acid winter sky was scraping the tops of the buildings, corroding the upper floors.

The Section Chief was talking again, his voice a low monotone, forming the words slowly, precisely. "I'm sure you all appreciate the importance of these reviews . . ."

L.'s mind was drifting once more. Important. Yeah, sure. To who exactly? Weren't they covering ground that had already been trampled to death? L. absently pushed the pile of papers away from him a quarter of an inch with his index finger: The Report. It was all there in great detail. Too much detail apparently. He had come under suspicion obviously, though of course they didn't say so.

There would have to be someone involved at the top. Someone with a special interest. On the surface it was just a routine low-level intelligence report. There were hundreds of thousands of similar reports filed every year. Who would bother to exhume this one once it had been consigned to the bottomless pit of government archives unless there was something of unusual importance at stake? It could only be someone who didn't view it as a routine investigation. A shadow agenda was being hinted at. It was both a warning and a threat.

Maybe these weren't the facts they really wanted. Maybe the facts he had dug up were inconvenient. Perhaps he had gone too far, assumed too much initiative. Deciding what the facts were was slippery business. There are always different criteria for choosing the facts depending on what you wanted them to prove. But what were they supposed to prove? Someone was looking for an advantage, or for cover. Everyone was entitled to their own opinions, but were they entitled to their own facts too?

The Section Chief turned his full attention on L. and was speaking again.

"You seem to have filled in a lot of blanks. The departure is significant, and in some ways disturbing. Where did this extra background information come from?"

L. cleared his throat and looked at the pile of papers in front of him. "The standard sources. The usual imbedded assets. Plus anyone associated with Mote on even the most casual level."

The Section Chief pursed his lips again. "I see." A long pause now. Again the silent disapproval. L. could feel the eyes on him around the table.

L. said, "I was instructed by ops to get beyond the bare facts and try to put them in context. To get everything I could that might relate to the missing file."

"Beyond the facts," the Section Chief interrupted.

"Well, perhaps 'beyond' is not the right word. To provide a background to the facts so they could be viewed against the arc of events as they unfolded . . . "

"Ah, an interpretation." A thin smile now.

"The facts remain unchanged. The sources are on record and have been confirmed—"

"Please, please," the Section Chief cut in sharply, looking more annoyed.

It hadn't been a good trip for Mote. Things started to fall apart right from the beginning. It was the special envoy's fault really. Needleman had his mind on other things apparently. Somewhere over Costa Rica he buttonholed Mote and took him to one side of the jet. Needleman was short, bald and had a shifty look in his eye.

"Look here, Mote, you get around a lot. You ever been to Buenos Aires before?"

Mote looked at him curiously. "Buenos Aires? Well, yes, a couple times."

"Know it pretty good?"

"Pretty good. It was part of the job."

"What's the nightlife there like?"

"Nightlife?"

"Yeah, you know ... the action. Places to go, meet people." Needleman was leering at him now. "Some broads ... Get lucky. You know what I mean."

Mote considered him before answering. "Well, I haven't been there in a while. Been a couple years now. Buenos Aires is pretty cool though. Friendly people. Some of the most beautiful women in South America."

"Great," Needleman said quietly, looking from side to side. "When we get there I'd like you to show me around. Leave those other bozos you're with at the hotel. Have them guard the luggage or something."

"I don't understand, sir."

"Call me Larry."

"I still don't understand, Larry."

"What's not to understand? I just want to get laid, doofuss."

"But we're not going to Buenos Aires."

Needleman looked like he had been struck with a hammer. He blinked a few times, gasping for air, his mouth opening and closing soundlessly like a fish. Then he cried, "What the fuck do you mean, we're not going to Buenos Aires?" He grabbed Mote's tie and pulled his face down next to his and hissed. "Don't give me any crap, you evil bastard."

Mote flicked his hand away casually. He was a head taller than Needleman. "We're going to La Paz … Bolivia. You're giving a speech there."

Needleman stared at him in disbelief, veins popping out on his forehead. "Bolivia!" he shouted. "Since when are we going to fucking Bolivia?"

Mote shrugged, placidly smoothing his tie. "Well, don't ask me. Ask Tweety Bird."

Tindal Bird was Needleman's special assistant. He was pear-shaped, gay, urbane and aggressively cologned. Everyone called him Tweety.

Needleman turned quickly and shouted, "Bird, get your ass over here!"

A practiced and guileful sycophant, Tindal Bird made it a point never to be too far away from his boss. Bird came flitting over with a flutter of hands. He had a crooked ingratiating smile and looked at them both in turn. He reeked of patchouli oil. "Goodness, what seems to be the trouble?"

"This asshole says we are going to Bolivia.... Is that true?"

Bird hesitated for a moment, then frowned and nodded slowly, trying to look solicitous. He hated to give Needleman bad news. "A cultural and geographical backwater to be sure. A miasma of failed politics, failed economics and failed ambitions. But unfortunately, it's all too true. That *is* our scheduled destination."

Needleman was wiping his forehead with his tie. "Jesus, do you always have to talk like such a fairy? How come no one told me this?"

Bird looked hurt. "Well I tried to tell you. Didn't I try to wake you up during the briefing by the State Department? I told you it was going to be important, but you just wouldn't listen."

"I can't stand those dick heads at the State Department. They all prance around like they got feathers up their ass. Why do I have to listen to a bunch of shit heads like that anyway?"

Bird shook his head and sighed. "A cruel twist of fate, Chief. But it's our job none the less."

"I know more about foreign policy than they do. You just tell the stupid bastards what you want them to do and pass out a few checks. That's how you conduct real foreign policy!"

"You're absolutely right. It's unfair. Most of them are retards. But we've got to make the best of it. Duty. Patriotism, all that shit."

Needleman stared at Bird miserably. Bird's hands were swooping around his head as he combed his hair with a blue comb.

"Goddamit, I wanted to go to Buenos Aires!" Needleman complained.

"Not this trip, chief."

"This really sucks!" He kicked Bird in the shins. "Now what am I going to do?"

Bird hopped backward on one leg, wincing. "All you got to do is give a speech. Jeezus, that hurt!"

"A speech! ... I don't have a speech prepared. ... How am I going to give a speech?"

Bird was rubbing his leg, looking like he might cry. "Shit. I don't *know*. ... Don't you have an old one you can use? How about that one you gave to the AARP? What's in your attaché case there?"

"Forget it. There's nothing there but sunscreen and condoms."

"Well, we've got to give them some kind of speech."

Needleman thought for a second. "I know, we'll have Mote here give a speech. Let me hear you say, the quick brown spic jumped over the Rio Grande."

"Me?" Mote took a few steps backward. "I don't know anything about foreign policy."

"You don't have to. You just go out there and talk. Say anything. Look here, you can read a few words out of *Sports Illustrated*. Those bastards don't speak English anyway."

"Forget it. It's your job, Larry."

"But I can't handle this. Don't you see I'm under a lot of stress here? I can feel my hemorrhoids popping out right now."

"Nope."

"C'mon, Mote, show some professionalism here. Your Head of Mission is asking for help."

"Sorry."

"I'll write a glowing report back to your boss. What's that moron's name?"

"No can do."

"How about a couple of Super Bowl tickets?... Forty yard line." His eyebrows were going up and down suggestively.

"Tempting, but still no."

"You're a cunning mean-spirited bastard, Mote. I'm afraid I'm going to have to suspend your beverage cart privileges for the rest of this mission."

Mote was unimpressed. "Get over it, Needleman. Have Tweety Bird here give the speech. Maybe he can throw in some pelvic thrusts that will explain our foreign policy better than words."

"Hmm ..."

"It's either you or him."

"What about the pilot? He's got a great voice on the intercom."

"He's too busy hitting on the stewardess."

"Okay, okay. I guess you're right. God, I have to do everything around here. Tweety, get your ass over here."

Tweety approached cautiously, keeping just out of shoe leather range. His voice was nearly a whisper. "I heard what you said."

"And?"

Tweety hesitated, looking coy. "I'll only do it just this

once. From now on you'll have to do it yourself."

"Good man."

"And I'm going to need a new wardrobe when we get back."

"Okay, anything. Just get your ass out there and try not to fuck up too bad. Clichés only. Don't get creative. And, Mote, you'd better wear a hat. That day-glo green hurts my eyes. Who does your hair anyway?"

Once they got on the ground it was apparent things weren't going to go well. The crowd of Bolivian shills, lured out by the promise of free baseball caps and ballpoint pens, had been milling around in the rain for hours. Most of them were pissing drunk by now, and getting belligerent.

When Bird and the others stepped up to the mike at the bottom of the stairs a taxiing jetliner caught them in the jet blast and blew all their hats off. The disoriented and confused mob let out a howl of appreciation when they saw Mote's green hair, thinking they were about to be entertained by some kind of retro-rock group. They began cheering and launching volleys of casquito bottles at their guests in appreciation. As the breaking glass crashed dangerously around them Bird's nerve gave out. "Incoming!" he shouted and scrambled up the ladder, followed by the rest of the beleaguered mission. Mote was the last one up the steps as bottles thumped against the aluminum skin, glass crunching beneath his feet.

Needleman screamed into the cockpit, "Let's get the fuck out of here before they wreck the plane!" The crowd had broken through the barriers and was shouting and climbing the ladder. Mote pushed the first one out of the doorway, took a bottle to the groin, but managed to pull the door shut and latch it.

"Christ, they're climbing on the wings now," Bird said.

"Go! Go!" Needleman yelled at the pilot.

"I can't," the pilot said. "You want me to run over these bastards?"

"Son, this is just like the Alamo. This is American property. Run over the sonovabitches!"

The pilot looked at him for a second, then shrugged. He nodded to the co-pilot, released the brakes and eased open the throttles.

They pulled away from the gate, the huge engines screaming, ignoring the frantic messages of ground control. The drunken Bolivians on the wings staggered, looked like they were dancing, then popped off one by one. They reached the end of the taxi-way then turned on to the main runway without stopping, opened the throttles, and started to pick up speed.

Needleman, visibly relieved, slumped into a seat. "Man, that was close. I need a drink."

Someone shouted, "Hey, look! There's still someone on the wing." They all rushed to the windows. On the port wing a tiny black figure, clothes whipping like mad, clung precariously to the leading edge as they accelerated down the runway.

"What should we do?" Bird asked.

"Maybe we should turn around," someone suggested.

"Are you nuts?" cried Needleman. "Abort the takeoff? Do want to get us all killed?"

The crowd all had their noses pressed to the windows. "Why doesn't he drop off?" someone asked.

"Looks like he got wedged in the air slot somehow."

The man, ripped by the winds, looked like he was struggling to find a better position. The landscape started to fall away in a dizzying rush as they gained altitude.

Bird had his nose pressed up against the cabin window. "Can't last much longer. I give him another minute max."

Needleman, watching the man too, disagreed. "I dunno. He looks pretty wedged in there now. I give him at least two."

"How much?"

"A hundred bucks."

"You're on," said Bird, holding up his watch, keeping one eye out the window. The man suddenly lurched into a new position. One arm was free. He looked like he was gesturing towards the cabin. "What's he doing now?"

"He's giving you the finger, Bird."

Bird looked offended. "Well, Jesus, that's rude! Like I asked him to be out there."

"Forty five seconds, Bird. And still counting!"

He finally fell off somewhere over Peru. He had lasted on the wing an amazing twenty-five minutes.

Needleman smoothly pocketed Bird's C-note. "Persistent little bugger, wasn't he?"

"I wonder where he hit?"

"I don't know. But it does make you stop and think, doesn't it?" Needleman had suddenly grown solemn. He looked around at the other passengers gravely. They all had ashen faces. He raised his hand then stepped up on one of the seats to speak. "People," he said, looking at each of them. "I think it's necessary for us to pause and reflect a moment. To pay our respects. Today we witnessed a human tragedy. Through no fault of our own, a Bolivian citizen has plunged to his death. We are, of course, all saddened by this awful, this terrible, turn of events. Yet, even in the face of our unbearable suffering, we must stop and admire the human spirit. Here was a man—though obviously stupid—who displayed how tenacious human beings can be in the face of adversity. Let this be a lesson to all of us."

Luckily for Mote, by the time they got back to Washington the Bolivian airport riot had escalated into a rebellion that threatened civil war. A marginalized group of politically committed revelers, hating to see a good party come to an end, decided to form a popular front and immediately marched on the capital to protest the corrupt military regime and the greedy multinationals who bled the country of iron ore and brought back basketball shoes in return. The national palace was sacked and some semi-important people were trampled to death, including the vice-president and his fifteen-year-old wife.

In the U.S. press the Needleman adventure was portrayed not as a fiasco, but as an ill-fated diplomatic mission of goodwill caught in a sudden outburst of violence by international terrorists bent on overthrowing the government and destabilizing the whole region. Mote, as the head of the security detail, was given a large share of the credit for their narrow escape. The Bolivian wing-walker was never mentioned.

● ● ●

The Section Chief looked preoccupied. After a long silence he frowned, looked up from the document and said, "Did it occur to you that these supplements might be considered a liability? For better or worse, they are memorialized now."

"I was given the assignment by operations to make a full report. That's what I endeavored to do. The question being considered was, did Mote play a key role or a minor role in what eventually transpired? At the time I had no way of knowing. It's still not certain. My directions were to gather as many facts … as much information as possible in case events took an unexpected turn."

The Section Chief stared at him with dead fish eyes. He had to be aware of the scope of his assignment. Why was he questioning that now?

The Section Chief slowly turned over several pages and pushed them aside as if they had an unpleasant odor. "I have to say at this point I am troubled by a number of things. Not least of which is the invidious nature of these portraits. It violates a number of standards which may relate to our professionalism, and our loyalty."

L. didn't say anything. Loyalty—obviously not to the truth. Professionalism—meaning partisan politics. This was not going well at all.

The Section Chief tapped his pen on the table and looked around the room. "I am going to seal this portion and hold it over for further review." The men at the table nodded their assent and turned over the section one after another. "Let us hope we find the rest less worrisome."

Of course he already knew what he would find. He had already read it through several times. Mote, Durwood, the missing Q file. What was the real agenda here? Somebody had screwed the pooch.

"Proceed."

No, he wouldn't explain it all, but Durwood was the common link. An idealist probably at the beginning, like so many others. His history turned out as bizarre as any of them. But first, before the Krenmeister debacle, he and Mote would share a desperate mission.

Talking Heads

The turning point for Bob Durwood came that day back in August. It was not unlike any other day for the staffs on Capitol Hill and the White House. The same small-minded politics and factional bickering. The same petty turf wars and back-biting. The headlines in the underground press and blogs came out that morning with yet another attack on the President. This was nothing new either. The few sources of news that had eluded government control were always whining about something, couldn't accept the fact the Constitution was irrelevant now, and the country had moved on. It had progressed beyond the need and encumbrances of primitive social bric-a-brac. Why couldn't they just get over it?

The day started off pretty much the same as any Monday. It would end far different for Bob Durwood however, a struggling unknown cipher in the government machinery, and lead directly to the Mote desert mission, a clandestine affair with a beautiful spy, and eventually into the secret heart of the notorious "Inner Circle."

The Undergrounds. How could you get excited about them really? They took on an importance they didn't deserve. They generated unbelievable paranoia and endless gossip considering their near total irrelevance. Bob didn't bother to read their tiresome litany of complaints, unlike most of the White House staff, who surreptitiously circulated the printouts among themselves and snickered over the embarrassing revelations and scandals at lunchtime like mischievous seventh-graders. The erratic little publications that daily savaged the Commander in Chief had only a miniscule readership among the general population. At least that's what the accepted media experts asserted. (It wouldn't be till much later that Bob would question the trust he automatically put in so-called experts.) Bob was convinced then that only marginalized social failures, the lunatic fringe, hopeless conspiracy theorists and other assorted nuts were the only ones who could take that stuff seriously. A waste of time. Why the staff read them and passed them around was a mystery to Bob.

As the main target for their attacks, El Supremo (that's what the big boys called him in the Inner Circle) loathed the underground press. Not that he cared all that much for the regular press either. He especially didn't like reporters who were semi-celebrities in their own right. Reporters who had the annoying habit of asking substantive questions soon found themselves sitting further and further towards the back during press conferences. Eventually they didn't even make it in the door and the grand viziers of the established media would quietly replace them with more administration-friendly types who could be counted on for "a more balanced view" and "more reliable commitment to the truth."

So far all El Supremo's efforts to stamp out the noisy undergrounds had failed. He simply couldn't find the sneaky little cockroaches that kept publishing all that shit on the internet. They kept moving around on him, never operating in one place too long. Even after firing the head of the FBI and replacing him with a saxophone player he still got no satisfaction. He was running out of patience, something had to be done. The staff was sweating bullets; high-paying jobs were at stake. His outbursts were becoming more paranoid and violent, bordering on frenzy.

Bob had just come out of his cubbyhole in the basement and was entering the commissary to get another load of coffee and doughnuts. He was scraping brown icing off his tie with a fingernail from the previous batch, thinking about last night's failed attempt to get into Corvetta's pants again. What was he doing wrong? He just couldn't figure it. She had grown distant lately.

Goldstein suddenly spotted him and came slouching over. Oh, no. Not this guy again, Bob thought miserably. "Check this out," Goldstein said, talking out of the corner of his mouth. Goldstein worked for the

Secretary of Commerce. He was wearing a bad tie, a wrinkled shirt and his usual conspiratorial air. Some men seem to know a lot more than they say, Goldstein was just the opposite. Goldstein always tried to give the impression he was privy to a lot more inside information than he could reveal. He gave Bob a quick look at the printout hiding inside a folded *Wall Street Journal* while he waited for his turn at the pastries:

Tone Deaf Tyrant Leaves Us Breathless!
Ten-Thumb's Plan to Strangle Basic Freedoms

Goldstein leaned close, flapped one eyebrow up and down like the handle on a broken toilet, and whispered, "Our fearless leader saw this and went psycho this morning. Totally lost it! Started chewing on the curtains."

Bob looked around anxiously. He didn't appreciate Goldstein's uninvited confidences and assumption of comradeship. He always had the uncomfortable feeling of being watched, recorded. Bob ran a forefinger around inside the collar of his shirt and said, "Well, they're always attacking him about something." He hoped Goldstein would find someone else to annoy.

Goldstein, eyeing the pastries, slipped in front of Bob with a practiced move and said, "The tyrant stuff and strangling basic freedoms he didn't give a shit about. Fuck that! It was the 'tone deaf' and 'ten-thumbs' part that sent him ballistic. Started gobbling like a turkey, drooled all over himself. Told the cabinet they were bunch of fucking idiots. Called the French ambassador a sniveling shithead!"

"Who told you that?"

"Dilworth, one of the security guys, witnessed the whole thing. Lost it big time I guess. Said the crazy bastard was fit to be tied." Goldstein busied himself spearing the last two cheese danishes then turned and winked at Bob significantly. "I had to laugh at that. Told him tying up a quadriplegic ex-guitar player couldn't possibly gain you much." He laughed suddenly like Porky Pig, slapped Bob on the back, and glided away with the pastries.

Bob watched his retreat with relief. He would make a point to avoid him in the future, at all costs. He was too dangerous, a loose cannon that talked way too much. Sooner or later someone was going to nail him. Didn't he know how things really worked, how they were always watching, recording, going through your waste paper basket, ceaselessly poking around, filing reports? Making disparaging remarks about the leadership and tasteless jokes about quadriplegic guitar players was a recipe for personal disaster. Especially when you considered El Supremo was the most powerful quadriplegic in the history of the planet.

• • •

Bob made his way back to his cubbyhole trying to understand what El Supremo was so excited about. It was only the underground press, after all, which no one ever read. Hadn't marketing people always said the only really bad press was no press? Come to think of it, no one even paid attention to the legitimate press any more, let alone the underground. So what was the big deal?

He decided to ask a staffer about it he saw being pushed down the hall—Lance Torino, also a quadriplegic and a member of the Inner-Circle. Maybe he shed some light on this.

A shapeless blob of meat with a few vague protuberances turned his way and some silver tubes fell out of his nose on to the cart.

Bob suddenly realized it was an impulsive act and totally presumptuous to flag down a member of the Inner Circle.

"Who is this cretin, anyway?" the squeaky little voice whined. His pusher, another Secret Service type with sunglasses and a permanent kink in his neck, grunted and humped him off down the hall.

• • •

"And you obtained this most colorful background portrait how?"

"A lot of leg work. The usual channels. Surveillance, paid informants, and in certain cases through some of our bureaucratic opposites. Not all of them are hostile."

"Indeed."

"Occasionally there's a reasonable amount of cooperation."

The Section Chief frowned. "One must be extremely careful enlisting cooperation."

Well, that was true. Investigations can always cut more than one way. "Sir, I understand that different agendas may be in effect, but the sources all seem to agree. I tend to think it's an accurate reflection. It probably resides more or less the same in many files by now."

"And why is that?"

"There seems to be a lot of interested parties. Lots of people would have the same access. Plus, it could be spun in many ways depending on the perspective."

Silence for a moment, then, "I see. ... And this Goldstein?"

"Nothing more there."

"Reason?"

"Dead. ... An accident I was informed."

A slight arch of the left eyebrow. Another pause now. The look of disapproval again. "Need I remind you dead men often do tell tales? Was his estate thoroughly vetted?"

"A couple agencies from the DOD and NCTC went over it. Then I dug up their several reports. They never found any evidence he was even marginally connected with the missing file. Still, his estate was sealed and his papers and possessions examined and cleansed before release to the heirs. Just as a footnote, there was some subsequent controversy about the validity of his will, or wills. Some family members mounted a legal challenge to the fact he left the bulk of his assets to an extended family of hamsters at an animal shelter in Lake Worth, Florida. It seems that towards the end insanity was closely dogging his heels."

What Next?

"Things are getting weird." Brimstone had said, looking up from his morning newspaper. For some people reading the Sunday paper was a form of relaxation. For Wilbur Brimstone it was a source of constant irritation he inflicted upon himself with the morbid fixity of a hopeless addict. Wilbur Brimstone was a professor of sociology at a university in Montana built next to a nuclear waste storage site.

Brimstone was right, things were getting weird.

"Don't worry, Dear," his wife said. "They'll get a lot weirder."

Brimstone was reading an article on the latest fashion trends and scowling ferociously. "Says here, style-wise quadriplegics are a hot item, and that fashion designers are copying their look. ... Can that be true?"

His wife shrugged. "Who knows these days, Dear?" she said dreamily. She went back to gluing the fin on her model rocket.

It was true. They were becoming hot. Some well-known fashion blogger had expressed the view that they had "a unique look and an unmistakable style." The social networks took it up from there. Everyone started talking about them. After years of struggle simply not to be pitied or patronized, they had suddenly become not only accepted by society, but style icons and models for imitation.

"What the fuck is going on here anyway? Does anyone

have a clue?" he asked Myrna Dempster the following Monday. Myra was the graduate assistant he was humping on weekends. They were in his office over the sewage disposal plant sorting through her prescription drugs, anything that might give them a buzz.

"Oh, you know, pops, the usual thing. Mass stupidity. Imbecilic behavior as an art form." She shrugged, looking bored. "Some loosely-wired avant-garde types looking for an angle decided they looked cool and started copying them. You gotta be different to stay in front of the pack. I was thinking about doing a research paper on it. But then again I thought, fuck it, who cares? You know, I might just go back to nail tech school."

Brimstone looked at her in amazement. "You mean people have come to the point where it's fashionable to imitate the severely disabled?"

"Absolutely, pops. It's the latest look. Profoundly cool. Total shock and awe factor. The real heavyweights are one-upping each other with their I'm-more-fucked-up-than-you-are routines. Getting real obnoxious in some cases, having themselves pushed around in wheelchairs, cutting in front of lines, demanding special attention at clubs and restaurants, that sort of thing. It's pretty amazing to see how people will willingly fuck themselves up just to be cool. On the other hand, I don't have much to brag about. I'm attending this dead-end college and getting banged by a fossilized old fart with halitosis."

Brimstone sighed. Sooner or later it had to happen.

"I wonder what those morons in the department think of my book now?"

In his book, *The Advance of Mediocrity*, an impressive piece of scholarship and erudition that sold 350 copies, Brimstone had seen something like this coming. The book was a catalog of dire predictions and stark warnings about the direction society was taking. In the introduction of his book he had written:

In a self-indulgent, mentally lethargic, and largely obese population, society and culture rapidly mutate into increasingly unrecognizable and dismal forms.

The morons he was referring to were the other members of the sociology department. The truth was that none of them had bothered to read his book. Most of them thought Wilbur Brimstone was a paranoid crank.

• • •

The Section Chief was sucking on a lozenge. He said, "Where do we stand with this so-called scholarly work?"

"It was difficult to find. I think one or more heads have copies of it. I located one volume on the internet. The individual who sold it is being detained indefinitely. Not officially because of the book of course. Other suspicious activities. We can always come up with something incriminating if we try hard enough, dig enough. Help things along if we have to. There are always options."

He was always amazed at how easily people could be intimidated. How easily they could be led to work against their own best interest, assist in the digging of their own grave. Maybe that's what really kept all governments in power. McCarty had put him on to Brimstome and his book. McCarty was big on history. Where others saw chaos, he saw threads in a complex unfolding tapestry, hidden patterns of cause and effect driving men and events.

• • •

Brimstone had become alarmed, recognized with growing apprehension the handwriting beginning to show up on the walls. When excrement encrusted canvases started being hung in major galleries Brimstone was horrified and immediately characterized it as a harbinger of more bad news. The explosion of the internet was speeding everything up, good and bad. Traditional standards were melting down on all fronts. Art was becoming unrecognizable, the various movements collapsing into chaos and irrelevance. Once the cognizenti had conferred masterpiece status on several glass jars of shit created by an Italian artist, guerrilla counter movements rapidly sprung up. Art forgery became rampant. Here was art even the untrained masses could produce on a regular basis (provided they were regular) in their own home that was virtually indistinguishable from the original.

Literature, taking it cue from the rapidly mutating texting generations, was becoming fragmented and unintelligible. Grammar, punctuation and even spelling had been deconstructed and increasingly falling into disrepute as being hopelessly last century and restrictive. Standards everywhere were crumbling like the polar

ice sheets. The once unthinkable had become accept-
able, then eventually even desirable, under the unrelent-
ing tsunami of instant global communication.

Brimstone, standing at the lectern of his Sociology 101
class, warned, "The lowest common denominator will rule
from here on out."

The students were unimpressed, "Yeah, and you're a
fucking old windbag," one of them shot back.

Brimstone sighed as a paper airplane struck him in the
forehead.

• • •

"Okay, okay! What's going on here?" Manny Diamant
shouted, flapping his arms like some fat bird. The assistant producer was in a foul mood again. He had arrived on
the set with his usual entourage of faggots and ass-kissers. "Where's that dumb ass director I hired?"

The crew all looked at each other but no one answered.
Finally one of the cameramen said, "Taking a shit."

"Tell him I want to see him."

The cameraman gave him a dismissive smirk. "You tell
him. I'm setting up for the next shot."

Diamant was ready to turn on him but then thought
better of it. He was paying these poor bastards way below
scale and couldn't afford any more defections.

"The shit I have to deal with!" he growled. He tramped
over the cables and through the maze of equipment and
props followed by his two pet nancy boys and a skinny girl

with a clipboard. They stopped at the men's room door. There were some loud, unappetizing rumbling noises coming from inside.

"Bruce, go in there and tell Krebs I want to see him," Diamant ordered. "Right now."

Bruce looked pained, hesitated for a second, then cautiously pushed the door open and went inside. The rumbling noises were louder, more ominous. There were two brown shoes visible under one of the stall doors. Bruce approached the door apprehensively and rapped on it lightly. "Mr. Krebs?"

"Beat it!" an angry voice inside boomed.

Bruce took a nervous step backwards. "Mr. Krebs . . . Mr. Diamant is here and wants to see you."

"Look, can't you see I'm busy? Go back out there and tell him I can only take one shit at a time."

Diamant was pacing back and forth, muttering darkly when Bruce finally came out looking slightly green. "Well?" Diamant demanded.

Bruce looked faint, he was breathing deeply trying to revive himself. Before he could speak the door burst open, knocking Bruce out of the way.

"Manny, good to see ya!" Krebs said, giving him his best car salesman smile. Before becoming a movie director Kaiser Krebs had been a car salesman and had set a company record for getting the most illegal immigrants financed.

"Forget the sweet talk, Krebs. I want to know why this movie is such a piece of crap."

"Crap?" Krebs said, raising his eyebrows.

"Yes, crap. There's no action. I've seen the dailies and it plays like some kind of goddam Finnish art movie. A bunch of boring butt-heads trying to figure out if they should scratch their hemorrhoids or eat some turnips."

"Surely you jest?" said Krebs gravely, standing up to his full six-five. "Pahlavi, your partner, our esteemed executive producer, said he loved it. This is based on a true story after all. Or at least a partially true story. At the very least a story that could have been true and you are willing to accept the fact the main characters are all total idiots with no redeeming human qualities whatever."

"The story sucks."

"Of course it sucks. It's an imbecilic script."

"Where did you come up with this goddawful piece of shit anyway?"

"You wrote it."

"I wrote it?"

"Absolutely. Don't you remember? You gave it to me a couple weeks after we started shooting when I suggested that we need some kind of script if we are going to do a movie. It's kind of an unofficial custom in the movie business to have a script. Until then we had just been shooting random shots. Street traffic, airplanes flying over, homeless people in the park. You said you wrote it in one afternoon watching football games."

"Well, I never expected you would take it so literally. A script is just a suggestion, a hint as it were. Don't we have some asshole writers to juice this thing up?"

"Can't afford 'em."

"Shit, we need to do something. This piece of crap

needs more action. Some car crashes, explosions, kung fu fighting, some violent fist fucking maybe. Any goddam thing."

"Too expensive," Krebs said, shaking his head. "I could have the main character let the air out of someone's tires."

"Not good enough."

"Have someone punch a hole in his screen door."

"Better. But still not enough."

"Leave it to me, Manny. I've got just the thing."

"What?"

"I'll find some poor sucker on the internet. There's all kind of talent out there you can screw for free. They'll figure it out."

"You think so?"

"Absolutely."

"All right. But it'd better be good."

"No problema, Manny. No problema."

Manny tripped over one of the cables on the way out and gashed his head on an electrician's toolbox. His staff carried him out to his car and stuffed him in the back seat.

Krebs took out an antacid and ground it up on his back teeth. "That guy is a real pain in the ass," he said to Larry, the sound man.

"Are you really going to look for a another writer?"

"Fuck no. This thing is beyond hope. Maybe we can turn it into a cult movie."

● ● ●

"Start right there."

"Where?"

"Where it's underlined."

"But I can't read this shit. It's all in pencil. Couldn't you have at least typed this out?"

"We didn't have time. Manny wrote it in the john while taking a dump at half-time."

"But I can barely read it."

"You'll be fine."

"You know, you really need a script editor. Or at least someone with a computer and a printer."

"Are you just going to bitch all day?"

"What's this word right here?"

"'Brimstone' . . . Jeezus, even I can read that."

"You've read it before."

"No I haven't. Just read, asshole. We're on a very tight budget."

"Wait a minute, what's this brown spot here?"

"Don't ask."

"Yeah, but it looks like—"

"Read."

"Okay! Okay . . . Ahem!"

(VOICE OVER)

As the American population grew ever more lethargic and obese, approaching 90% in the middle of the 21st century, he announced the spiral down was picking up speed. Brimstone could only grind his teeth in despair when the bloated shapeless mass of guilty couch potatoes he excoriated for their self-indulgence were suddenly let off the hook psychologically by a new book by Denise Blimpton, *I'm Not Too Fat, You're Too Skinny.* The book, written in one afternoon by a Dunkin' Donut clerk, rocketed to the top of the lists. It was followed immediately by a sequel, *Girth is Good,* which was an even bigger success. Doublewides everywhere breathed a collective sigh of relief knowing they weren't really out of shape after all, once you redefined 'average' and adjusted the mean upward.

The movie industry, always with its ear to the ground for cultural trends, decided to make features with increasingly tubby heroes and heroines. Fatsos quickly struck box-office gold. Bloated and misshapen protagonists were taking Hollywood by storm. They now had the "look." Industry marketing analysts also discovered a parallel trend—fat was good, but fat and ugly was even better. No more chiseled features and lantern jaws for this generation of moviegoers. They wanted reality now, warts, cellulite and all.

Fashions soon followed Hollywood's lead. The sleek, sexy looks of the last century gradually slid into baggy shapelessness. The runways of New York were filled with women factory workers from Eastern Europe strutting their considerable stuff. Professor Brimstone, a born conservative averse to change, noted with alarm that hideousness in all its shapes, forms and manifestations was rapidly becoming the universal standard for emulation. A new value system was radically changing the aesthetic judgments and sensibilities of the country. "The classical Greek models will soon be gone," Brimstone complained. "When they go, things will not be pretty . . ."

"Cut!"

"Jeezus, where did you get this mike, the dollar store?"

"Larry, how'd that sound?"

"We picked up some background noise. Someone farted I think. You want a retake?"

"Naw, forget it. I don't know if we can use it anyway. Manny didn't write this shit. He ripped it off somewhere. Sounds like some freshman term paper. That illiterate bastard couldn't write a laundry list."

"I'm still going to get paid, aren't I?"

"I was going to put it in during that montage where the tour bus crashes into the nursing home. But I don't know now."

"Hey, look, I got bills too!"

Brimstone was right, things were getting ugly, and it was worse than he imagined. But Brimstone didn't live long enough to see the Quad Thing develop to its dismal conclusion.

While returning from a conference, taking a ferry boat from Brunswick to St. John's, Nova Scotia, someone reported seeing a whale on the starboard side. The tubby American tourists on board, startled at such news (whales had been thought to be extinct), rushed en mass to the starboard rails. It was like a stampede of overweight elephants and the boat suddenly capsized. Ironically, the only two fatalities were Wilbur Brimstone, who couldn't swim, and a woman from San Diego who was inadvertently harpooned by a confused Eskimo from Miami who was hunting in a leather kayak. According to reports, he was there on vacation and was attempting to get in touch with his roots and had tricked himself out in traditional Eskimo gear. Unfortunately, during his years as an investment banker next to the Orange Bowl, he had lost some of his native hunting savvy and mistook her for a sea lion. The whale that supposedly had been sighted turned out to be an abandoned oil tank someone had dropped into the water.

"I told you things would get weirder," Brimstone's wife said, gazing misty-eyed at his fading photograph on the mantle. It had taken her nearly a year to get up the courage to gather all his old clothes and shoes together to give to the Salvation Army. The shoes were the hardest part because they still retained the shape of his feet exactly, as though he was still standing in them, a ghostly presence who seemed to be waiting for something. She had started to talk to his various pictures on the mantle periodically, updating him on the latest news he would find particularly interesting—or annoying. She felt at times he was actually there in the room with her, listening and slightly aloof, not answering, but nodding patiently as if in confirmation of his theories. Sometimes at night she thought she could hear the faint scratchings of his pencil as he wrote out his books and articles in longhand on yellow sheets of legal pad.

● ● ●

McCarty poured himself another brandy and said, "There is still some mystery as to who was the first truly serious copycat quad. Several have claimed the distinction. Disfigurement as a way of showing group solidarity has been around since prehistory. The tattoo era was hideous enough, but this is something entirely new and incredible, self-immobilization as a fashion statement."

At first, the idea was dismissed as just another insane California fad—some weird new publicity stunt by a few of the brain-dead fringe groups the country was producing in ever increasing numbers. But when some avant-garde, media savvy types began picking up on it in New York and Los Angeles, elective spinal surgery had suddenly become a political statement and an outrageous new strategy for standing out in a crowd. The seriously cool saw it as a daring display of personal style that would leave their peers thunderstruck, and instantly set them apart from the common herd. "It was an ultra-radical move, but that was the whole the idea," Bob Charmin, a record producer in Miami, told a reporter, "At least you aren't a boring run of the mill slob anymore like everyone else. When I roll into a club in South Beach now I get noticed in a hurry."

"But is it really worth it?" the reporter inquired thoughtfully. "I mean what about pussy?"

"Are you kidding?" Bob said. "Most American women would love to have a man in my condition."

"You mean totally helpless?"

"Absolutely. Once I let a broad push me around for a while, I'm in like Paco . . . Right, babe?" He glanced over his shoulder at a lissome blonde. She smiled vacantly and wheeled him over to the bar.

The Quad Thing was more than just trendy. It ignited heated controversy. The blogs sites and social media began weighing in on it—both for and against. People discussed it over water coolers, behind pizza counters, in unemployment lines. Brimstone would have quickly recognized it as something more pathetic and venal: a potentially profitable career strategy.

Apart from the advantages of style, it was a calculated and cynical patriotic affirmation, demonstrating the individual's trust, loyalty and absolute dependence upon the state. And therefore a neat way to cash in, basically. To a large segment of the American population, already mostly inert and mentally anesthetized, the idea of having all your needs looked after by someone else—the government—had a strong appeal, especially to many of the more parasitic elements. It was a long term insurance policy. Didn't the state, after all, have infinite resources for the unquestioning patriots who identified with it entirely and supported it unconditionally? You could always squeeze the older working stiffs a little harder, cut back on giving bums and homeless people money, most of whom just weren't with it anyway.

"I'll bet you never thought it would go this far, did you, Dear?" Mrs. Brimstone said softly, a big tear rolling down the end of her nose. She wiped it away with a tiny handkerchief and touched it to the glass.

• • •

The Section Chief looked annoyed. Maybe he would call an end to it for the day.

"Did this Brimstone factor into the subsequent events as anything more than background?"

"Directly there is no evidence. He did have some impact though. Hard to tell the precise measure. Q was an admirer according to rumor, and owned a copy of his book. We've identified some snatches and fragments from it in random postings on the internet. Data mining and the like. Hard to judge its staying power in the long run. Certainly something to be aware of and continue to monitor. It gained almost no notoriety when it came out. Only a few copies were ever published, and most of those were remaindered. But I think everyone knows how these things may be rediscovered and propagate long after their apparent demise because of the net and a few fanatics. Even after being thoroughly discredited and quashed by the Publications Quality Control Agency, sometimes these things can linger."

• • •

"This is old news of course, but you must understand the background and know the forces at work," McCarty had said, smiling wanly. "Things don't happen in a vacuum. History accretes, snowballs, and begins to acquire momentum of its own apart from the individual players. Knowing the plot points of history is the only thing that can protect you. Your role as a pawn is to be sacrificed. You must visualize the real game going on below the surface so the apparent one becomes intelligible."

History up close can be preposterous, he went on to warn him. That doesn't make it any less dangerous. Or less devastating if you are caught on the wrong side of it. McCarty had a keen appreciation for human folly and viewed it with relish. "If the previous century has proven anything, it's that the general citizenry will tolerate and accept anything, no matter how grotesque or despicable, with enough propaganda. Society needs drama."

"Like suicide bombers."

"The amazing thing about suicide bombers is not that there are people willing to blow themselves up because some mental incompetent wearing baggy pajamas says it's a good idea. The amazing thing is that there seems to be an endless supply of them. So when you think about it, is it any more amazing that people would disable themselves then blow themselves up as a human bomb?"

It didn't take long for the Quad Thing to catch on once it was given the stamp of approval by society's cooler members. These were the usual geniuses of self-publicity and media hype who become important celebrities, and are usually imbeciles in any other context. As a career option for a young impressionable generation of TV and computer addicts, the attraction could be powerful. They didn't do anything but lay around all day anyway. This at least spared them the depressing burden of trying to get a low paying dead-end job. Of course, taking a shit sometimes could be a problem, but then you can't have everything.

Entrepreneurs quickly saw an opportunity. Low-budget cord snappers were rapidly setting up shop in malls and abandoned health clubs around the country, offering free tattoos and wheelchairs as an added inducement. Sociologists at Michigan State University claimed it was the long overdue reverse swing of the pendulum from the excesses of the Health, Fitness and Face Lift generation.

Montana Fenwick had started it all. He was the catalyst and the inspiration behind this radical and alarming new trend. As with any cult figure, fanatical devotees will often go to extremes trying to copy and identify with their hero. And it was all because of a nearly fatal accident.

Montana Fenwick had been an international rock star with a huge following, and an even bigger ego. He had made his way from a garage band in Lansing, Michigan to the top of the music world with his band, "Dead Nutz." The group's ear-slitting music explored the darkest nether regions of structureless high-decibel dissonance. One enthusiastic reviewer described the sound as "something like a steel mill being hit by an atomic bomb, only a lot louder."

He was at the peak of his career when tragedy struck. After taking the stage one night against the advice of their manager during a rainy outdoor rock concert in New Orleans, right at the end of the concert, a sudden bolt of electricity arced between his Gibson Stratocaster and some loose wires. The resulting blast left him sprawled on the stage, a smoking, hairless pile of fried meat. The crowd immediately went nuts, thinking it was part of the awesome finale that usually included huge and dangerous explosions. Attendants wheeled him off the stage on a cart, through the cheering crowd, and into a waiting ambulance. One of the two fans they ran over as they peeled out of the parking lot died later that night. It was the kind of concert legends were made of. T-shirts with bloody tire treads were immediately a hot item and prized souvenir. His fans didn't realize until later their hero was now completely inert.

Depression set in. Music just didn't get it for him any more. Totally bald, unable to think with any consistent clarity, he decided on a career change that would fit his current capabilities almost perfectly.

"I'm running for President of the United States," he announced to his cheering fans at a press conference in Los Angeles.

The voting population, most of whom had grown up listening to his albums (many now stone deaf), swept him into office by a large margin. Or so it was reported. In truth he also received some valuable help from some hacker friends who tweaked the electronic voting machines.

If there were two things Montana Fenwick (now known as El Supremo among the Inner Circle) hated, it was rainstorms and bad press.

And, of course, there was always Quattlebaum . . .

—————— **Diligence Rewarded** ——————

Bob watched the line of ants making off with the last few crumbs of his doughnut. It was quite a long line, down the side of his desk, across the floor, and out the door. He wondered how they got in. The housekeeping was getting a little slack. It was later that same afternoon, after his encounter with Goldstein in the commissary. He was sitting in his office trying to figure out what he was going to do for the rest of the day. He had been on the President's legal staff for six months now and hadn't been given any assignments yet. He hadn't even been able to figure out what his job was really. The legal staff seemed heavily bloated already, judging by the number of people marching up and down the halls not looking particularly busy.

He had been hired straight out of law school on the recommendation of the dean, a former staffer himself, and handed the keys to an office. He hung around every day from eight to five mostly playing computer games or watching the government TV channel in order to keep up to speed on what was happening inside the beltway.

The office was located in the new basement addition of the White House and didn't have any windows. In truth, it was pretty much a hole. At one point he had gone out and bought some small picture frames for his desk with the intention of brightening things up a little bit with some family photographs. Once he got his photos out and compared them to the ones that came in the frames, he decided he liked the looks of those people better than the ones he had, and put his own back in the desk drawer.

He flipped through the channels on his wall TV. It could have been yesterday's news, the usual menu of disasters and tragedies. The ozone hole was still getting bigger. Miami and New Orleans flooded again, the polar caps turning to slush. The twentieth year of drought in Africa. A gang of teenage cigarette smokers killed in a shootout with Chicago police. And there was Krenmeister again, giving another speech on the senate floor. Bob settled back and turned up the volume. Looked like he was really working up into a lather today. He was pounding the podium again, waving his arms. Krenmeister was the President's point man on the new breathing laws El Supremo was ramming through Congress, a mostly absentee body of venal ex-lawyers. Krenmeister was the perfect majority leader. He was tough, ruthless and had no discernible scruples. His best quality though was his flexibility. He would come down on the side or any issue whatever at the drop of some cash. His harangues at this point seemed like overkill since political resistance to the proposed mandatory neck meters for the apathetic population was inconsequential at best.

As El Supremo had shrewdly guessed, public opposition had been little more than some ineffectual grumbling by a few disenfranchised liberals. It had already been swept aside by the marketing pros and the national media who controlled public opinion on behalf of the administration, the major corporations and their own self-interest.

"Citizens with nothing to hide have nothing to fear," Krenmcister said. "Let me state to our citizens that these measures are in the best interest of everybody," He always delivered it with just the right amount of patriotic fervor and moral certitude. Bob knew it by heart now. (Here Krenmeister would usually pound his chest with one fist and look to the heavens.) "These laws will protect our precious air and our freedom to breathe it. It is our sacred responsibility to preserve this vital national resource by monitoring and regulating it for the benefit of all our citizens and for generations to come."

Bob yawned. Was he watching yesterday's news? No, he had a different tie on. Different tie, same message. He had heard all of Krenmeister's rants before. Goebbel's law of repetition. Repeat something enough, and, well … you know.

It was working exactly as planned. When the bill was introduced, there had been a flurry of partisan controversy—all superficial and thoroughly choreographed for the media by the Tweedle-Dee and Tweedle-Dum parties, complete with numerous opportunities for sound bites. Whether or not it was an insult to personal freedoms for citizens to be required to wear neck meters was barely discussed. Who cared about that anyway? It was painted as a national security issue, and consequently off-limits for debate or serious discussion. Fear is government's best friend. Public security always trumps personal freedom, no matter how bogus the threat. You were either for it or you were a possible subversive, a potential terrorist, someone perhaps that after some close checking could be declared an enemy combatant and could be disappeared.

The ambitious plan had only one flaw: implementation. That was the real problem. Technically it wasn't as easy as first supposed. Monitoring and taxing air usage in someone's home or workplace was no trouble. It was a relatively simple job to attach meters to the exhaust vents of buildings. That part had been easy and was already raking in nice profits for the Wall Street backers of the plan.

Taxing personal usage outside was a different matter however, and had been significantly delayed. The mandatory neck meter every citizen would be required to wear (after paying a hefty licensing and registration fee, of course) was about the size of a cell phone with a collar. In fact, it was part cell phone—one of its chief selling points. But the self-adjusting collars were plagued with difficulties. During testing sometimes they would tighten up for no good reason and choke the unlucky volunteer to death. Sabotage had not been ruled out. The Chinese manufacturers denied any wrongdoing. They claimed the engineering was totally American, and if they were flawed then it was America's problem. Heh! Heh!

Bob yawned again, louder this time, and flicked the

last crumb off the desk to see what the ants would do next. Just then Mona Clutch popped in the door. Mona was the blonde pool secretary for the underlings like Bob. She had a tight little ass she liked to shake at the male staffers whenever the opportunity presented itself. She always wore a bunch of metal bracelets that made her sound like a wind chime when she moved.

"Just thought I'd warn you, Bob, Red Tercel is on his way to see you."

Bob looked up, surprised. "Tercel? You sure he's looking for me?"

"Positive. Asked where your office was."

"Maybe they're finally going to give me something to do."

"Or fire you." She smiled brightly for a second, cracked her gum, then said, "See, ya." She turned and clinked out the door, giving Bob full benefit of her jiggle.

Red Tercel, still fully ambulatory, was front man for El Supremo's chief of staff, Fred Loop. Loop was the feared gatekeeper of the Inner Circle, and tightly controlled all access to the President. Bob re-knotted his tie, stood up and re-tucked his shirt. Might as well look tidy if this was going to be his last day. He was just zipping up his fly when Tercel barged in the door.

"You Durwood?"

"That's me."

Tercel looked around the office and frowned. He had a big square head with shaggy blond hair and was wearing a rumpled suit.

"Geez, how do you work in this dump, Bob? I'm Red

Tercel." He stuck out a big paw and pumped Bob's arm. He was one of those power grip guys who liked to get a small workout whenever they met someone.

"It's not so bad once you get used to the insect life. What can I do for you?"

Tercel sat on the edge of the desk and dangled a foot and stared at Bob like a fat barracuda sizing up a small fish. "For me, nothing at all. But maybe something for the President. That's why I'm here."

"You sure you got the right guy?"

"Is there more than one Bob Durwood here?"

"Not that I know of."

"Then I got the right guy." He leaned forward suddenly and picked up one of Bob's pictures off the desk. He studied it for a second. "Good looking group you got there. Fine looking wife, nice kids."

Bob smiled uncomfortably, hoping he wouldn't notice the price tag and the company's logo on the stock photo he had covered up with a felt marker. "Er … thanks."

"Obviously some good genes there. My family looks like a bunch of mutants. Not very photogenic like yours." He put the frame back down on the desk. "Oh, well. Wouldn't change 'em for the world though. I respect a good family man." Bob knew he had three ex-wives and four kids, three of them in jail for sex offences.

"They're my pride and joy," Bob said, beaming.

"Anyway, the reason for my visit, Bob, was to introduce myself and ask you to come up to the Elliptical Office tomorrow. The President wants to have a chat with you. May have a little job for you. Ten sharp." He stared at Bob for a while as though appraising some sort of specimen, then slid off the desk and looked at his watch. "Oops. gotta go."

Bob tried to hide his confusion. "May I ask what this is all about?"

Tercel smiled enigmatically. "You'll find out then, Bob. See you tomorrow. ... Oh, and don't be late. He hates that."

"Thanks. Mr. Tercel," Bob called to him as he went out the door. He could see a bunch of squashed ants on his butt.

Bob sat there motionless. It took a few minutes for it all to sink in. He suddenly gave a little whoop and jumped up from behind the desk, pumping his right arm like a piston. This could be it, he realized with growing excitement. The Big Enchilada he had been looking for all through law school and his brief professional career. As the least senior attorney on a heavily bloated legal staff, he couldn't help but think his star had taken a sudden and dramatic rise—all the more sweet for being so unexpected.

Bob spent the rest of the afternoon in a daze, shuffling and reshuffling the same papers, preoccupied with the possibilities. This was obviously something big, but what could it mean? He said something about a little job. But why would the President want to see him? He didn't think El Supremo even knew his name, let alone would honor him with a face-to-face.

At exactly five o'clock he locked up the office, took the elevator to the parking garage and queued up to wait for his car. It was starting to rain by the time they brought his gray little plastic box around. He squeezed in, punched the nav coordinates for home and was soon swallowed in the weary stream of monotonous gray traffic groping through the murky atmosphere.

He couldn't wait to tell Corvetta the news. Not many people got to meet with the President. Not many people got to meet with the Red Tercel for that matter, who had come down to his office personally. Maybe this would change things between them a little. She had been so distant lately, so preoccupied. They had been married a year and a half now and she seemed like a different person. She was more demanding now, more critical of little things he did. Their lovemaking had fallen off drastically. She always seemed to find something to be angry about just before they went to bed.

Broken little cars and debris littered the shoulders. The rammers were busy today. One of them thundered by him on the left, a huge armored diesel powered machine with an angled blade on the front for blasting dead cars off the road and onto the median or beyond the shoulders. The flimsy, expendable cars died in droves along the highway like flies on a window sill. The rammers punched them off the road so traffic could keep moving.

The rammers were the kings of the road. Every kid wanted to be a rammer. The huge machines could be murder in the wrong hands. A psycho in Florida got his hands on one and went on a rampage, killing 232 people on his way from Boca Raton to Orlando to attend a Baptist convention. The air force finally had to take him out with an air strike on I-95. Corvetta's girlfriend, Emily, who lived three floors above them was a rammer. Come to think of it, she had a little psycho in her. A great body, but nuts all the same.

The little car exited the expressway as programmed, logged off Traffic Control Center, and returned control to Bob. Two hours and eighteen minutes. It was taking longer than ever to get home. Too many high-rise condos now lined the route, their gray faceless occupants plugging up the roads and the exit ramps with all their cars. Too many crappy fourth-world on-board computers crashing and snarling traffic for miles with backups.

Bob tried to spot his building up ahead. He was close now, only about a quarter-mile. Home was one of those gray new gigantic mega condos like all the others he had just passed. A brownish yellow haze, drifting in towering ominous formations, hid it from view.

He had bought it at a good price through a friend of Corvetta's who was a realtor and lived on the same floor. The building itself was 116 stories tall and covered two square blocks. It was the latest in "new concept" housing units. New concept meant ultra-high efficiency housing that maximized every possible cubic inch of space. By doing away with the traditional concept that all housing units should have exterior walls and windows, developers were able to pack a lot more units under the same roof and inside the same wall area and make a lot more money. True, they were just big ugly boxes, warehouses really, but they certainly were cost efficient. Actual windows, which they now proclaimed obsolete, were a thing of the past. Insurance companies hailed the move as architecturally progressive and far-seeing since the walls now had no glass to break. They rewarded their customers by raising the rates for homeowner insurance. Real windows were replaced by virtual windows, LCD screens that could be programmed to any view you wanted. Bob usually had his picture window looking out over the Beagle Channel in Tierra Del Fuego.

He found his usual spot on the ninth level of the cold and gloomy sub-basement and took the elevator up to the lobby. Vandals had smashed the lights again inside so he rode up in the dark, glass crunching under his feet. It smelled like someone had peed in it too. The lobby was empty except for Fred the security guard sitting at his desk.

"Identification." Fred said, putting down a tooth-marked sandwich.

"Fred, it's me, Bob. I've only lived here a year and a half now."

Fred wiped his mouth on the arm of his shirt and let a fart. "Rules are rules. Do you want me to leave this place unprotected?"

"How come the lights are always smashed in the elevator?"

Fred shook his head, looked bored. "Not my problem. Call management."

Bob fished out his ID and slid it across the desk. Fred studied it for a minute. "What's your business?"

"Same as usual, Fred. I'm coming home from work."

"Go on up." Fred belched and scribbled something down on a grimy clipboard.

Bob said, "You're doing a great job, Fred.... By the way, you have a piece of bologna stuck in your teeth."

Bob unlocked the door with three separate keys. Corvetta was standing in the middle of the room and completely naked except for two sheets of paper, one stuck to each breast with a piece of cellophane tape. She was looking at herself in a wall mirror, turning this way and that. The bank of TVs was running, all six tuned to the same twenty-four hour all-execution channel. They were injecting someone in Texas again. His eyes were as big as saucers as they poked around for a vein. They looked like they were about to fly out of his head.

"Nice outfit," he said, putting his briefcase down on the couch. He looked closer at the two pieces of paper. They were life size color photographs of massive breasts. There was a stack of similar photographs on the coffee table.

"I'm trying to decide," she said without taking her eyes off the mirror.

"Decide what?"

"Which ones I like the best. Dr. Gupta sent these over for me to check out. I didn't realize there were so many choices… Pointy… Pendulous… Perky."

"I like the ones you have now. Why do you want to change them?"

She thought about it for a second, then frowned. "Right. It's always about you, isn't it? … Well, what about me? What about what I think?"

"All I said was I like the one's you have. If they ain't

broke why fix 'em?"

She glared at him. "I could expect someone like you to say that. You just don't get it, Bob."

"Hey, it was a compliment," he said hopelessly.

"Some compliment! Like you're saying, it's okay you have little tits. I forgive you. I don't mind your short-comings."

"Whoever said you had little tits?"

"Doctor Gupta. He said for a woman of my height I should have slightly larger breasts to be aesthetically correct."

"This is ridiculous. I think he's ridiculous."

"He's the leading boob man in the state. He handles the boobs of celebrities from all over the world."

"That's great. I think he should keep his hands off your boobs though."

She tossed her head, swinging her blonde hair back. "Sometimes I just can't believe what a jerk you are ... You know, I think I like the pointy ones. They're kind of aero-dynamic." She had a different set of boob pictures stuck to her chest now.

He said, "How about one baggy and one pointy? That'd be cool."

"Yeah. right. ... Moron."

Bob shrugged and let it go. He picked up the remote and turned to the bank of TV's. He flipped all the selec-tors to random.

"Hey, I wanted to watch the twitching part."

"God, how can you watch that stuff all day?"

"What should I be watching? Boring educational shit?"

"I don't know. Just seems a little morbid."

"These people are scum. That guy tried to strangle a TSA agent who was only feeling his crotch for explosives. They're getting what they deserve. As a big shot government lawyer you should know that."

The room was suddenly filled with a crowd of people as the channels clicked in: talk shows, shopping, televangelists, Nigerian investment opportunities, pyramid schemes, government talking heads. Bob went into the kitchen and made a couple of iced drinks and brought them back out.

"Here, a peace offering," he said, holding one of the frosty glasses out to her.

"Go ahead and take it. I've got some good news."

A Room With A View

He was supposed to meet El Supremo at ten, but arrived at the outer office a few minutes early in order to check in with Fred Loop, the chief of staff and key member of the Inner Circle. He was on a motorized bed with his head propped up on a pillow. His bed had a little aerial with a pennant on it. Bob recognized it as Harvard's coat of arms. He had been the first of the Inner Circle to be surgically 'initiated'.

"Lousy mood today," Loop warned, frowning. "No joking at all costs."

"No problem. I don't know any."

"Good."

It was another hour before he got to go in. He went through the massive carved doors, crossed a savannah-like expanse of ankle-deep blue carpet, and stood in front of a gleaming black desk that seemed as long as a city block.

El Supremo had his back to him, horizontal on his hand tooled, adjustable Lay-Z-Dude bed, looking out through the mullioned windows at the smoky lawns and dead leafless trees, apparently lost in deep thought.

As he approached the desk and first saw El Supremo, Bob was awestruck, imagining the enormous weight of responsibility resting on those surprisingly thin, flaccid shoulders. It was strange and a little frightening. Here in this unprepossessing shapeless, even grotesque, mass was the exalted, mythic focus of power for hundreds of millions of people, each trusting their fate to the benign, all-powerful embrace of the state. It was ironic that the man behind all this, the man who bore the weight of this crushing responsibility, the man who's visionary leadership of the administration that had relieved the confused citizenry of the tiresome burden of making decisions for themselves, should seem so insubstantial and frail in the flesh. He seemed to exist only through the force of his indomitable will. Bob's eyes began to mist over.

At this point El Supremo cut a couple of quick farts. Nothing showy or particularly presidential, just a couple little paint peeling stinkers. He turned suddenly to Bob, the bed rotating on its axis. It was controlled by the pressure from his long, prehensile tongue, coiling wetly over a control box with red buttons. He seemed surprised to see Bob standing there, and quickly pulled his tongue back inside like a retreating moray eel.

"Well?" he demanded, eyeing Bob suspiciously.

"But you invited me, sir. I'm Bob Durwood, assistant staff attorney. Ten o'clock. The Elliptical Office—"

"Quit blithering, Durwood," he cut in sharply. "Do you know who Morton Quattlebaum is?"

"No, sir."

"You should. He has committed grave offenses against this office. The very presidency of this great and powerful nation … What do you say to that?"

Bob stood speechless for a few seconds. "Well … The laws are quite specific as to offenses against this office, Sir. I suggest prosecution to the fullest extent."

"You're a fucking genius, Bob."

"What did he do exactly, sir?"

El Supremo's lumpy looking face worked its way into something approaching a smile. The tongue oozed out of its hairy cave and mashed one of the buttons. "Bob, you've got a lot to learn. A whole lot. Do you like whiskey?"

Bob was still overwhelmed, still trembling slightly and would probably have accepted a glass of piss at this point. It was the start of his personal relationship with El Supremo, his introduction to the secret and powerful world of the Inner Circle.

"What kind of person is it that doesn't mow his lawn?" Mrs. Kavelitch was quoted as saying in the report. "He didn't mow his lawn, or even wash his car very much. Now what kind of person is that? We all try to keep up the neighborhood standards, but he didn't care at all. Not that he wasn't nice enough when you talked to him. In fact, he saved old Mr. Dumbowski's life once by reviving him after a heart attack. But still, I never trusted him. Anyone who can't mow his lawn on a regular basis has got something wrong with him. I'm glad you people are investigating him. There are too many deviates on the loose already."

Bob put the FBI report back in the file with the green tab and turned to the next item. The stack of folders was nearly three feet thick.

"You'll see that every item in there confirms the conclusion the he's a terrorist and a psychopathic criminal," El Supremo said. He sipped the whiskey noisily through a straw.

"Not mowing your lawn is only a misdemeanor," Bob pointed out somewhat reluctantly.

"I didn't mean that one, goddamit! I thought that was the one where he wrecked the CIA computers by turning all their files into gibberish."

"Maybe this is it," Bob said helpfully, pulling out another overstuffed file marked 'Secret.'

"Never mind," El Supremo said irritably. "That's just one small item. It does show a certain consistency though. A blatant disregard for the opinion of others. Read the rest of that pile. It's all in there. Enough to curl your hair. The man is a danger to civilized society. A terrorist of the worst kind. You'll see exactly what I mean after you read the rest of it."

Bob studied the mountain of documents in amazement. The various intelligence agencies had done their work with gusto. There were records and reports on Quattlebaum going back to the time he was in second grade.

"I didn't realize it was possible to get so much information on one individual."

"That's nothing," El Supremo snorted through the whiskey. "There's three more cartons of the stuff outside. ...But you look a little puzzled, Durwood. What's the problem?"

"No problem, sir. ...I was just wondering if you could get this much information on the average citizen. Someone who's no threat at all."

"Damn right we can. But if you've got nothing to hide, you've got nothing to fear. I think Thomas Jefferson said that. A free country requires an intelligence service second to none. One that's not afraid to cut the balls off any anti-American bastard. Your job is to bring yourself up to speed as soon as possible and report back here with a plan for nailing this guy. They tell me downstairs that you've got brains. I want you to prove it to me."

Bob nodded and started to stand up, assuming their meeting was over. He wondered who told him he had brains.

"Oh, one more thing." El Supremo said. "I want you to see Morganfliess after you go through all the crap in those boxes"

"Who's that?"

"NSA. She's he only one I trust over there. The rest of them are a bunch of career suck-asses who will tell you anything. She can fill you in on a lot of background. Grew up in the business. Extremely bright. Dad was a station chief. Speaks five languages. A little erratic at times. Writes poetry. Wanted to be a folk singer once. But hey, who gives a shit, right? I was an artist once. We all make mistakes."

"Yes, sir."

"I want a report on my desk every morning about your progress. Get it?"

"Yes sir."

"Good luck. Good hunting. And get that bastard for me!"

"Yes, sir."

"Now beat it."

• • •

Bob left and carried the two big cartons of papers down to his cubbyhole. It was just the tip of the iceberg El Supremo said. He wondered what he was getting himself into he thought as put them on the desk and closed the door.

It seemed too weird that El Supremo would call on someone he didn't even know to try to find Quattlebaum when he had the entire intelligence community at his disposal. You didn't ask questions of the President though. Then again, maybe he was being set up for some kind of sacrifice. Maybe some kind of patsy was needed as a ritual offering to get someone else off the hook for some nameless deed. He certainly had all the right qualifications for that roll: lack of experience, unquestioning loyalty. A desire to please superiors? Yeah, even that. But what was wrong with that? That's the way the world works. That's the way you have to play it if you want to be anything in this world. He would have to be careful, keep his eyes open for danger. Still, there was no choice.

He did not want to turn out like his old man who wound up selling mud flaps at red lights in Laredo.

The Desert Rat

"Turn, you slimeball! Turn!" Conrad Mote was shouting. Bob went white as they hurtled through the air sideways, then landed with an explosive crash that blew out the back window. The suspension groaned and began popping, threatening to come apart as they wallowed out of the sand.

Ahead, Quattlebaum led them on a snaking course through the twisting valley. He was rapidly running out of room—and for the first time he hesitated. He backed off the throttle momentarily, and seemed uncertain which way to turn.

"Go for it!" Mote pleaded, pounding on the wheel. At last Quattlebaum made up his mind, cranked the wheel hard left, and gunned the engine. He flew into the narrow gorge, tires spinning.

Mote gave out a whoop. "The mistake we were looking for!" He jabbed the nav-screen with his big thumb. "Look, it's a dead-end. We got him. We've finally got him!"

They careened over the rocks, dodging the granite outcroppings. The saw-toothed edges of the mountains grew higher and steeper as the canyon narrowed and the road grew more treacherous. In the pitching mirrors Bob could see the snouts of the rest of the pack close behind, snarling and bucking in their wake. Dust and smoke from Quattlebaum's machine billowed over the hood.

"Can't see," Mote grunted.

Bob's facial ticks blossomed into wholesale spasms when Mote decided to compensate for the lack of visibility with some extra velocity, and punched it to the floor. Huge boulders whipped by inches from Bob's head.

The right front fender exploded off the car as they grazed something solid. "Lousy goddam econobox," Mote complained, deciding it was time to savage the gearbox once again. Dust was now inside the vehicle too, pouring in through a gaping hole in the floorboard.

"Mote!" Bob screamed, "Mote, it won't go any faster, you fucking idiot!" He had his head pulled down inside his shoulders, his hands covering his face.

Deaf in one ear from Quattlebaum's hand grenade, Mote thought Bob was encouraging him to pick up the pace. "I can't go any faster," he shouted over the noise.

A second later the other front fender was gone, ripped off the chassis and spinning far into the desert. "Wooo! . . . Did you see that?" Mote said admiringly, twisting around in his harness. "Hey, what the fuck's the matter with you? You look like a turtle or something."

Bob thought he was going to be sick.

Mote stood on the brakes, sliding to a halt. Their deceleration was aided emphatically by a huge boulder that smashed the radiator and starred the windshield. A vehicle piled in behind them, then several more. Air support was chattering excitedly on the radio.

"Out! Out!" Mote was yelling, unfastening his seat belt. "This is it! We got him cornered."

Bob scrambled out, bruised and aching, into the swirling dust and smoke. Overhead, chopper blades were pounding the air, whipping the landscape into a blinding tempest.

"Back off with the choppers!" Mote screamed into a hand held radio. "We can't see a thing down here."

The helicopters edged back and Mote hurriedly positioned his men in the rocks. When the dust finally drifted off there were fifty guns leveled at Quattlebaum.

He didn't seem to mind a bit. He was sitting on the hood of his car, smoking a cigarette, looking slightly bored. Bob watched him through the glasses as Mote and the others inched their way forward cautiously.

"Hands on your head," Mote bullhorned. "Lie face down!"

Quattlebaum ignored him and continued smoking. He

was tall, had black hair combed straight back, and was wearing a silver jacket and sunglasses. Mote and his men, all wearing camo outfits, advanced in short, coordinated rushes until they were within thirty yards of him.

"Face down on the ground or we shoot!" Mote ordered. He was enjoying himself now. Quattlebaum threw the cigarette down but made no effort to move from the hood.

"Ten seconds, asshole!" Mote boomed.

Quattlebaum seemed to laugh, and shook his head sadly.

The first two bullets shattered the windshield. The third and fourth hit him in the chest. After that they came too fast to tell. The heavy slugs blew him off the hood and kicked him over the desert floor like a rag doll, shedding limbs and parts along the way. Bob watched in eerie fascination. He had never witnessed anything like this before. He twisted the focus ring, following the corpse as it disintegrated under the rain of gunfire.

"Hold it!" Mote shouted through the bullhorn. Something was wrong. "Cease fire!" The gunfire died out with a few last pops. Mote threw the bullhorn down angrily and bounded over the rocks to the twisted silver jacket. "Bastard!" he said, kicking it violently. A spray of metal parts flew out and glittered in the sand.

Bob put the glasses back in the case, dusted himself off and slowly picked his way down through the prickly pear cactus. He glanced at Mote briefly, then went to the car window and peered inside. The printer on the console was running. He waited until it finished, then peeled it off.

"Here, Mote, must be for you." He couldn't help but

smirk when Mote snatched it from his hand.

> *Gentlemen:*
> *Congratulations! You have just snuffed out the life of Rodrigo Quattlebaum II, a collection of silicon, aluminum, fiberglass and even a little duct tape—all in all a rather crude collection of elements. Might I suggest the next time you are looking for an adversary to match wits with you choose something less of a challenge, something perhaps on the vegetable level. I understand that about fifty miles south of here there is a bunch of unruly cantaloupes that have been occupying farm land, refusing to move, or identify themselves. I'm sure if you pool your collective intelligence you can come up with enough brainpower to defeat them in a pitched battle—provided of course you have sufficient air cover.*
> *Regards,*
> *Quattlebaum*

• • •

"I see from your c.v. that you worked with Mote in the past. Is that correct?"

L. said, "We were in on the same criminal investigation. That was before my signing on with the agency."

The Section Chief turned over a page on the top of the pile and worked his eyebrows up and down. There was the faint hum of air-conditioning in the background. The murky ochre atmosphere outside reflected faintly off the polished desk.

Well, so what if he worked with Mote before? Mote was just a plain cop in those days. They both were. They were both ordinary foot soldiers who had come up the hard way. Had both seen better opportunities, or at least better money, in the intelligence community. It certainly didn't affect the report one way or another, or his mission. Mote was involved incidentally, but he wasn't the point...Or was he? There were always murky undercurrents you weren't aware of in this organization, linkages that were hidden out of agency necessity or personal self-interest.

Maybe there was more to Mote than met the eye. Maybe he was carrying more baggage than he knew. His string of dubious assignments certainly hadn't come out of a vacuum. They had been made at higher levels all along, and perhaps had different motives than he thought. Could it be that his frequent lack of success was the result of having to pull both ends of the rope?

The Marvin Zipsky affair, though the police closed their files on it, was never satisfactorily resolved from the agency's standpoint. He knew that because he had made a special point to see it. The file had never been properly put away, and had been yellow-tagged for further review. That was carried over too.

Marvin was, of course, no threat now. But was Marvin's death even the real focus of the investigation? There were a lot of loose ends out there that had never been tied up. Some of the files had intentionally, or unintentionally, been compromised. By whom?

It was an odd piece of business all the way around. Absurd even. But maybe that was planned too. Your past never dies, but the truth of it rarely survives. Governments have always known how to use it as a resource. McCarty again.

How many years had it been now? It was hot that morning he remembered. The sky was like dull metal and there was a Santa Ana wind blowing in Los Angeles, rattling the windows, putting everyone on edge. Thinking back on the details now, it seemed like part of that bad movie again.

The Zipsky Affair

Marvin Zipsky had always been a mess. His life to that point had consisted mostly of bad whiskey, cars with bad transmissions, and a string of bad decisions. It was late morning and Marvin Zipsky sat his Pabst Blue Ribbon on the coffee table and frowned at the day's mail. Not a single check. He had been expecting a check from the insurance company for his phony back injury, but there was nothing but a couple motorcycle magazines and a fat brown envelope. He looked at the envelope. The return address, neatly printed, announced it was from his mother.

Funny, he couldn't remember his mother ever using a

computer or even a typewriter before. He belched suspiciously, wiped his mouth off on his sleeve, and pulled the flap open. It was Marvin Zipsky's last bad decision. Tearing the paper released tension on the mousetrap-type spring, which struck the detonator. The classic letter bomb detonator. The explosion blew the top of his head off.

"Messy!" Police Lieutenant Conrad Mote said a few minutes later, poking at some smoking wreckage with the toe of a size twelve. They were the first cops on the scene. They had been eating lunch just around the corner at Harry's Open Pit Barbeque when it blew. Mote still had the remains of a sloppy-joe tucked in his coat pocket.

"Careful, Lieutenant, You're standing on some brains."

Mote scuffed his shoes off on the sculptured carpeting and fished around in his pocket. "Know what this reminds me of?"

"What?"

"The Dorfmann Bombing. Just like this. Ten to one the guy's a vegetarian."

The place still smelled of high explosives. L. tried not to look at what was left of the headless Marvin. A nose clung precariously to the edge of a bloody TV cart. He'd seen some rough stuff before, but this was repulsive. Mote was less squeamish; he still considered himself technically on his lunch hour and happily finished off the remains of his sloppy-joe. He began looking for something to wipe the barbecue sauce off his hands. The drapes would do, he decided, and was proceeding nicely when a flashing piece of metal suddenly ricocheted off the coffee table.

"Holy shit!" Mote cried. "Incoming!"

L. could still remember the blind rush of panic that day. The cold fear. This little part of the adventure was left out of the report, of course, and the one delivered to the Section Chief. There seemed to be more to Marvin's death than the police were led to believe at the time. Were there fingers reaching into the investigation even then? Some other players involved? It was too bizarre. Or was it? Everything connected with Mote seemed to lead off into surreal worlds. Working for the agency had taught him there are always easy answers, but rarely good answers.

Mote dove behind the cheap vinyl couch and started digging like a raccoon. Sweaty, heart-thumping seconds passed as they waited for the blinding flash and a final lights out. But the blast never came. It wasn't another bomb after all, only a lousy beer can. They both breathed nervous sighs of relief and looked up to see it had come from a hole in the ceiling. The hole, still smoking around the edges, was about the size of a manhole cover, caused by the vicious little blast that took Marvin out.

Upstairs, just visible through the shattered floorboards and broken plaster, a man was drinking beer and staring off into space. They could hear the frenetic sounds of cartoons on television. The man was in his fifties, wore a ripped t-shirt, a three-day growth of beard, and a resolutely vacuous expression that seemed to indicate he wasn't the least bit concerned that a large hole had suddenly appeared in his living room floor. He belched happily, cracked open another beer, and tossed a cigarette butt into the conveniently located new hole.

Mote snorted angrily and bulled his way out from in back of the couch. He snatched up the beer can in his huge paw and crushed it into a ball, then stood in the middle of the room glowering up through the hole. He held the can at his belt, checked over his shoulder, and decided to work from the stretch instead of a full wind-up. The cannon shot struck the hapless Looney Tunes aficionado just over the left eye, dislodging him from his chair. They heard a howl, a rapid scuttling of feet, a door slamming, then the sounds of Bugs Bunny playing to an empty room.

"Split fingered fast ball?"

Mote nodded, pleased with his aim and the knowledge he could still deliver the high hard one if he had to. They went back to work. Mote began searching for evidence in the refrigerator.

"Hmm, pizza...With pepperoni. Well, the guy wasn't a veggie anyway. But I still say it looks like the Dorfmann Bombing."

"Yeah, but motive? We won't run into one like that for a while."

"Who's talkin' motive? I'm just saying it looks like the Dorfmann case to me."

It had been six months then since the Dorfmann case had come to its tragic conclusion. Mote was in on that one too. He seemed to have a nose for action, a talent for trouble. Maybe that's why the agency recruited him.

Denny and Lenny Dorfmann, publishers of the militant vegetarian newslettter, the *Broccoli Barb*, had quarreled violently one evening over some missing asparagus spears. Lenny accused Denny of giving them to a circus pinhead named Juanita, who he had been trying to seduce with presents of linoleum and vegetables. Denny angrily denied the theft and later smashed a Dove bar on the back of Lenny's neck while he was watching Judge Judy. Lenny, hot tempered and violent, returned fire with a spinach salad, and a full-scale battle erupted.

At some point in the melee Lenny lost a tooth. A little later he lost consciousness when Denny connected with a perfectly aimed Cuisinart machine, nailing him behind the left ear. When Lenny regained consciousness several hours later he found himself strapped to the exhaust fan of an Outback Steak House—left to be turned into jerky by his diabolical vegetarian brother.

Two weeks later the whole thing had been patched up and apparently forgotten. Then, one night, Denny was alone in the kitchen defrosting some brussel sprouts when they suddenly detonated, launching him right out the window. He hit the pavement five stories below in a shower of glass and singed brussel sprouts. "Ouch," he said, and died. Investigators concluded the brussel sprouts had been rigged with plastic explosives by Lenny, a former army demolitions expert in Afghanistan.

At his trial Lenny broke down and admitted everything, then promptly raised both arms and detonated two sticks of dynamite strapped to his armpits. The blast also took out his defense counsel, the prosecuting attorney and an unidentified female with a very small head wearing a sun dress made entirely of swirled linoleum.

"Oh, oh!" L. was in the corner crawling on his hands

and knees. "Take a look at this!" He held a burnt scrap of paper pinched between two fingers. Mote came over and stood next to him as he read it aloud: "*Hope you get a bang out of this! Signed, Your Mother.*"

"Crap!" Mote said. His muddy eyes were popping out of his head, his jaw working fiercely. "This pizza tastes like crap!"

Back at headquarters, the department's top-echelon thinkers rolled into high gear. They were led by the shrewd and often abrasive Major Horace Palderman, still considered one of the top intellects on the force even though a recent accident had nearly cut short his brilliant career. While staking out a construction site, hoping to personally nail a key figure in the rackets, he had inadvertently let a cement truck back over his head. Against all odds—and a great many hopes—he had made an amazing recovery, but occasionally got confused now, and would wind up standing in a corner for long periods until someone retrieved him.

"What about the letter, sir?" L. inquired.

"Straight to the heart of the matter. I like that, Sergeant. You could have a fine career ahead of you. Just watch out for cement trucks."

'Yes, sir."

"It was a cruel hoax, Sergeant," Palderman explained gravely, coffee dribbling down his chin. A photocopy of the charred remains of the letter were spread before him on the desk. "I saw through it immediately. A clever ruse, intended to make him think it was from his mother. And when he opened it . . . BA-BOOM!"

Palderman emphasized the decapitation part by slapping himself violently on the forehead. Another one of his annoying little quirks since the accident—dramatic hand gestures. Unfortunately, the effect was compromised somewhat by the fact he was holding a chocolate doughnut in his hand at the time.

He retreated from the office picking pastry shrapnel off his coat, gratified, none the less, to hear what official thinking was on the letter. He had been suspicious about the note himself.

The FBI had their own ideas about Marvin's death, however. They had ransacked the place then quickly taken over the whole case because explosives had been used. Other agencies were getting involved. They were trying to keep a lid on it too. The next day that they learned that something bigger than Marvin was afoot.

"They arrested some Iranian melon vendor in Chicago," Wilitski said. Wilitski was from bunko and had a lot of connections in the Bureau. "According to my sources, he's been under investigation for a whole string of bombings."

"Leave it to the FBI," Mote said.

"They say he blew up a trailer park in Florida, a Taco Bell and a National League umpire."

"Probably in on that conspiracy to blow up Congress too." Mote observed, picking his teeth.

Apparently they had a fairly big one. In addition to being a minor league terrorist, he was the suspected leader of a crooked trucking syndicate trying to muscle its way into control of the lucrative mud-flap industry in New Jersey. Crucial links had been established between him and Marvin—they both liked garbanzo beans and had the same hat size.

"How does that link them together?" L. asked.

"I dunno."

Not even the brilliant Palderman could say either.

Informing Marvin's next of kin of the crime was now the only piece of the case they had left. The Bureau had taken everything else. They had more important things to worry about. It turned out to be a problem too. Mrs. Zipsky was Marvin's only surviving relative and couldn't be located. Rumor had it that she had been stashed away in some nursing home, perhaps out of state. No one knew where exactly.

L. went through the usual procedures, checking out all the neighbors. They weren't much help. Marvin was thoroughly despised at the Kropotsky Apartments and nobody would talk to him, except under duress.

"A disgusting man. A living encyclopedia of odious traits," Mrs. Detweiler, his neighbor, assured him, a mass of pink rollers festooning her head.

Her opinion was seconded by Otto Kobasniuk, a turbulent Ukrainian living in the apartment next door. Otto hated Marvin with a homicidal fury. Over the course of the last two years, Marvin had somehow managed to burn Otto on the face with a waffle iron on three separate occasions. Because of Otto's excitable nature, and an idiosyncratic brand of English bordering on gibberish, he never did find out how Marvin accomplished this astounding feat. The only thing he could determine for certain was that Otto was now going through life with a permanent grid pattern embossed on his face. A fact that did little to improve an already grumpy disposition.

An anonymous phone call finally solved the problem. It was a piece of luck rather than brilliant police work, but then he wasn't looking any gift horses in the mouth either. It was a woman's voice, and there was the sound of music in the background.

"Go to the Happy Clam Retirement Home, two-twenty South Terminal Street. Room three-twelve. Do you know where that is?"

"Across from three-eleven."

"I didn't think you people were too bright. Do you have a pencil?"

She gave him the directions and he wrote it all down as quickly as he could on the cover of an old magazine. "Who is this anyway?"

"Never mind," the voice said, and hung up.

The Happy Clam Retirement Home was out past Watts in a featureless gray building set well back from the street next to a commercial laundry and a row of warehouses. A fat nurse in the lobby eating a bagel directed him up the stairs and down a long hallway that smelled of disinfectant to a tiny room next to the stairs.

He found her sitting on the edge of the bed reading an oversized book titled, *Great Moments in Rumba Dancing*. L. introduced himself and sat down on a hard wooden chair next to the window. She closed the book carefully and looked up at him with a pair wet brown eyes.

This was going to be difficult. He cleared his throat and said softly, "I'm afraid I have some bad news for you,

Mrs. Zipsky."

Her eyebrows raised slightly. "What is it?" she said. "Speak up! My batteries are down."

He hesitated a moment before speaking. "Mrs. Zipsky, Marvin's dead.

"Dead?"

"Yes. Someone blew him up last week."

She put the book down on the bed carefully, and looked out the window over his shoulder. He had expected an immediate and total collapse, but she seemed quite composed, was taking it amazingly well. Finally she shrugged, looked at him and said, "So what?"

He was a little taken aback. This was not the reaction he expected. "I have to admit you're being very brave about this, Mrs. Zipsky."

"Thanks."

"You don't even seem too surprised."

"Why should I be surprised? Marvin was a rat. That's why I did it."

"Did what?"

"Blow him to smithereens. What did you think I meant?"

He studied her for a second, then nodded sympathetically. Poor old thing was flipping out on him after all. Out of touch with reality. Alzheimer's probably. "Okay, Mrs. Zipsky, just try not to think about it."

She looked at him sharply. "Don't patronize me, flatfoot. I was the one that wasted the sonovabitch. He was a rat. He brought me here and abandoned me like some old derelict. Then drove off in my vintage red Coupe DeVille.

Told them I was senile because I liked to sleep in it."

There was obviously more to this than he thought. He took out a little book and a pen, ready to take notes. "Wait a minute, why were you sleeping in your car?"

"Why not? It was nicer than the Kropotsky Apartments and that idiot Kobasniuk living next door. Lots of people sleep in their cars. Did you know Mahatma Ghandi used to sleep in his car?"

He had to admit that he didn't.

"I got all the stuff right here." She handed him a copy of *Commando Monthly.* It was a magazine for mercenaries, professional assassins, international terrorists and accountants with vicious streaks. It was published in Davenport, Iowa. Besides complete instructions for making a bomb, they had given her a jar of black greasepaint for darkening her face on dangerous jungle missions.

He leafed through it while she explained some of the finer points of installing detonators. It was fascinating stuff. This month's lead was "Bludgeoning: Martial Arts Moldavian Style," by Metcalf 'Bullets' Bondini. According to Bullets, this ancient sport of kings (and some goat herds) was invented during the Middle Ages by Moldavian noblemen who couldn't afford swords or other expensive metal weapons, but still wanted to taste the glory of mortal combat, Basically, it consisted of beating each other to death with large pieces of lumber.

Bullets even gave a set of rules in case you wanted to try it out with some friends in your backyard.

He put the magazine down and studied her carefully. Some agonizing reappraisal was in store back at headquarters. Not to mention the FBI. This was going to top the Dorfmann case.

"We can't let you get away with this, Mrs. Zipsky."

"I should hope not," she said, yawning.

"It's a very serious crime you've committed."

"I know." She lit a cigarette and blew a couple of smoke rings.

"You don't seem very worried."

She shrugged. "I'm an old woman. What can you do to me?"

She was shrewd, this one. "Well, it'll probably mean the slammer for you."

"I doubt it."

"You're in big trouble anyway. They won't let you live here anymore."

"Big deal. This place sucks" she said, picking up the rumba book again. "Wanna see some real dancers, Sergeant?"

Mrs. Zipsky was defended by Richard Bolander Clark, Attorney at Law. Mr. Clark was young, successful, and arrogant to the point that he thought most of his clients were morons—which in fact they were. He didn't mind that they were morons though. He knew that you could make a fortune figuring out the legal implications of all the blunders morons committed.

He would defend Mrs. Zipsky for nothing. Richard Bolander Clark was no fool. He knew the value of publicity. And the Zipsky Bombing Case would certainly have plenty of that.

He hoped to get her off scot free, an accomplishment that would catapult him to the big leagues as far as state trial lawyers were concerned. His strategy was the classic legal defense—based entirely on bombast and chicanery. It was hampered by only one small detail—Mrs. Zipsky herself. She couldn't keep her mouth shut. She admitted she was guilty, and cheerfully bragged about it to anyone who asked her—and quite a few who didn't.

The trial itself had all the qualities of a three-ring circus. The District Attorney strenuously objected when Mr. Clark attempted to bring in a pair of midget acrobats, a juggler and a talking dog to testify in Mrs. Zipsky's behalf.

The verdict was reached only after several mistrials and numerous threats of contempt against defense counsel: not guilty by reason of insanity.

It wasn't exactly what Mr. Clark had hoped for; but it still got him a lot of publicity.

Mrs. Zipsky took the insanity ruling with equanimity. "Insanity is a damn sight better than senility," she told reporters, waving cheerfully as they whisked her away in the back of a station wagon.

A few weeks later Mrs. Zipsky was sentenced to the state mental hospital for the criminally insane. This was just fine with Mrs. Zipsky too. She smiled at the reporters again and gave them a jaunty thumbs-up as she was driven away in the police van.

"You know, Lieutenant, what I couldn't figure out is why she didn't keep her mouth shut. No one suspected her. Even the FBI thought the letter was bogus. She could have just walked." He was reading about it in the paper the next morning down at headquarters. There was also an article about the hospital where she now resided. "It's got to be this guy DiMazzio's group rumba therapy. Says here the director of the whole place, Dr. Guido DiMazzio, won the World Rumba Championships back in 1999."

"Crap!" Mote said.

"No, honest, Lieutenant, it says so right here."

"These donuts taste like crap. That bastard Palderman takes all the good ones; I saw them on his coat."

• • •

He had kept the full report in his own files and turned in a sanitized version to the agency, knowing they would have the flawed FBI copy already. Mote was just a nameless foot soldier and would make an easy target if someone needed to be sacrificed. The Section Chief was taking his time about it. It was getting late though. He would have to put his cards out pretty soon if he wanted to make it home for his evening cocktails.

The Section Chief cleared his throat and pushed the entire pile away from him. He looked like an unhealthy toad in an expensive suit that didn't quite fit. Ah, here it comes at last . . .

"I don't think I need to express to you that in spite of the sheer volume of your submissions, the key piece remains unaccounted for."

The Q file. How many people now were looking for it besides him? He knew his agency wasn't the only one. He was scaring up too many spooks, encountering too many roadblocks set by professionals. Finding the original unedited report written by government employees shouldn't have been this difficult. Something was seriously wrong. The fact that it was missing and the three men who had written it were now all dead was enough to make anyone suspicious, and nervous.

The Section Chief continued, "I must say I am becoming increasingly alarmed and severely disappointed by your lack of urgency. This is a matter of overriding importance and I would like to know when can we expect a resolution of this affair."

"The document is obviously more than just a threat analysis—"

The Section Chief cut him off. "Its contents are irrelevant. Its acquisition is all that needs concern you."

"I'm working on that now."

"And your progress thus far?" The voice was acid.

"The documents in question have a troubled history. They were obviously not lost. They were removed for a reason. I'm making arrangements to have them located and acquired."

McCarty had tried to warn him. McCarty, the big red-faced Irishman who had recruited and trained him, had told him the most important thing in this job was covering your backside. And you had to look at every assignment as an exercise in accommodating special interests primarily and national interest incidentally.

Robbins and Kleigman, both stiff-necked snotty types that hid their incompetence by talking tough, had given him the assignment.

"Do we even know if this file still exists?" he asked.

"It exists."

"How do we know?"

"Portions of it are being leaked on the internet."

"By who?"

"Would we need you if we knew?"

They gave him a background file and turned him loose. It wasn't much to go on. The three men who had written the original memorandum were all dead. Two died in a plane crash. (An accident?) The third disappeared in his boat during a storm somewhere between the Bahamas and West Palm Beach, Florida. He would have to find some way to develop his own leads.

Desert Redux

Now we go back to the desert again.

Durwood was looking at Mote distastefully, wondering why he had ever accepted a ride with this lunatic.

"We almost had him," Mote groaned, picking cactus spines out of his pants.

"Not even close, Mote."

"I can't figure how he switched it on us."

"The story of your life, pal."

"Now what?"

"I don't know about you, Mote, but I'm outta here."

He took the first flight back. He would hit the files again, look for his own clues rather than be pulled along by idiots like Mote and the Secret Service.

Luckily, it wasn't his plan. Never had been. El Supremo had ordered him along at the last second to help out if possible and get his feet wet in operations. The best thing to do now was to totally disassociate himself from these incompetent assholes. He had struck out badly this time. He wouldn't do it again.

There were no military flights available so he took a commercial flight back to Washington the next day. He didn't like flying in baggy smocks, but with the ongoing war on terror what could you do? No personal clothes were permitted on board and you had to wear an airlines issued outfit for each flight. An elderly looking man with a mustache sat next to him. After takeoff the man winked at him and said in a near whisper. "You know the only difference between taking an airline flight and being arrested is they don't put you in handcuffs."

Bob studied him for a second, looking into a pair of sad blue eyes. Oh, great, Bob thought. He was going to have to sit next to some crackpot bleeding heart liberal the whole flight. "Look, pal, this is the freest country in the world and we have to protect those freedoms."

The man smiled wistfully. "Keep telling yourself that. You just wait. The handcuffs are coming next."

Bob pointedly snapped open a *Wall Street Journal,* took peremptory control of both armrests, and looked intent.

•••

L. stood in the shadows of the alley watching the second story of the apartment building across the street. A light mist haloed the street lamps on the deserted sidewalks. He had been there two hours already. A cold wind blew down the alley. Something was moving in the corners, rats picking at the garbage, feral cats stalking the rodents. They were getting on his nerves. He would give it another ten minutes then leave, get something hot to eat.

A drunk, or maybe it was a drug addict, in a baggy coat and a large shapeless hat came shuffling down the street, lit periodically by grainy circles of light from the street lamps. L. eased further into the shadows. The man stopped a few yards away from him, then took a couple steps into the alley and stood next to the wall. L. could hear a trickle of water, then the sharp smell of urine reached him.

"I thought I taught you better than that," the man said in a low, raspy voice, zipping up his fly. "Wait here five minutes before you follow me. The cameras in this sector don't work but you still need to wait." The man turned and walked across the street.

L. waited as directed, looking up and down the street. A patrol copter went by very fast, lashing the street with wind. Its lights were pointed at the next block over. The door to the lobby had been left wedged open with a pencil. He removed the pencil, pocketed it and took the stairs up. The hall was dark, in need of paint. A thin line of light from the cracked door led him to the right apartment. He went inside and quickly shut the door.

"You look like you could use a brandy, my boy," the

man in the alley said. He was rummaging around behind a small fake bamboo bar. McCarty looked older now, more rumpled. How long had it been? Three years?

L. took off his coat and put it on a chair. The room was run down, the carpet threadbare and dirty. What the hell was McCarty doing here?

The old man put two tumblers of brandy on the counter and smiled sadly. "Rather a change from the last time you saw me, I expect. At least I have windows. A lot of people don't have that now."

"How did you know I was there?"

"There's a brick wall at the end of the alley. It has a tiny hole in it about the size of a bullet. It lets through a little point of light from the alley beyond. Something that wasn't there before had moved in front of that point of light." He handed L. one of the tumblers. "Always be aware of your surroundings. Remembering tiny details could save your life."

L. took a pull of the brandy and sat on one of the rickety bar stools. At least he still bought good brandy. "What happened, Mac? I remember Rolling Glenn. Why this dump now?"

McCarty took a sip of the brandy and smiled. "Hard lessons, my boy. You're never too old to learn them. You have to be careful about the friends you make. You have to be careful about who you put your trust in. I would guess that maybe you're at such a point right now."

"I don't know about that. But I did come for some advice."

"The Q file?"

L. looked at him sharply. "You know about the Q file?"

The old man swirled the drink around the glass. "I still have some contacts, some friends out there. It's a tight little good ole boy community once you've been in it for a while. The department heads live in glass towers with assholes manning the doors to keep them out of the loop. The truth is there aren't many real secrets amongst the old hands. Secrets are the currency of intelligence operations. If you want something you have to give something."

L. said, "Robbins and Kleigman ordered me to track it down. Gave me a file full of crap that's no help at all. Those ass-kissers want to see me fail."

"Naturally."

"So what do I do now?"

McCarty smiled wanly. He took a long drink and said nothing.

"No, really, Mac. What should I do?"

Mac stared at him without moving. Finally, he yawned and said, "Advertise."

———— Country Within A Country ————

Bob spent several days going through the files, then called Heidi Morganfliess at NSA. He had set up the appointment with Morganfliess' secretary. She said Morganfliess had been expecting the call and got security clearance for him and a pass.

He went through a bank of metal detectors and other various sensors before he got into the main lobby. The guard inside the NSA building eyed Bob suspiciously. He looked like a strip club bouncer. He was wearing a skinny blue tie that looked way too tight for his thick neck and made his eyes bulge. He gave the impression of an irritable guard dog on a leash.

"What's your business?"

Bob could hear a tiny whirr and a soft click somewhere over his head. A camera, rotating, recording, obviously. Must have been a cheap model, or in need of lubrication if it made that much noise. Bob told him he had an appointment with Heidi Morganfliess.

The guard grunted, stabbed a few keys on the terminal. He picked up the phone.

"Confirm M slash five-five, omega, red seven."

Everyone was big with tough-guy security codes here, Bob noted. The guard punched some more buttons, spoke some more gibberish into the phone, and kept Bob waiting for about ten minutes. Eventually he pulled out a plastic badge and handed it to Bob.

"Keep this on at all times."

"Bob looked at it before he peeled the back off and stuck it on his coat. It already had a picture of his face on it, plus a close-up of his retina.

Another beefy guard with a stone face and a similar skinny blue tie walked him to the bank of elevators and took him up to the 59th floor. In the hall secretaries and military types marched purposely up and down on important missions to save the world. The guard stopped at a gray featureless door just like all the others.

"In there," he said. "Don't go anywhere else in the building without permission."

"Not even to pee?"

"You'll need an escort."

Bob smiled at him and went inside. There was a secretary's desk, a couple of computer terminals and a lot of bookcases filled with what looked like bound reports. There was no secretary though. A door to an inner office stood ajar. He went over, tapped on it a couple times then pushed it open warily. A woman in her thirties was standing on a chair with a rolled up file folder in one hand. She had auburn hair and a tight little ass packed into white slacks like two scoops of vanilla ice cream. Bob stood in the doorway as she slapped at the wall then turned and lightly hopped off the chair.

"Bugs," she said, looking at Bob. "This place is filled with bugs. You'd think in a place like this they could at least keep the bugs under control. You must be Durwood."

"Right."

She studied him for several seconds with penetrating blue eyes. "So what do you think?"

Bob stared at her blankly, "About what?"

"About my ass. I felt your eyes on it when I was standing there."

Bob could feel himself turning red.

She said, "Never mind. You ready to go?"

"I just got here."

"That's okay. We're just leaving. You're buying us lunch."

"I've already eaten."

"But I haven't." She took a camel color purse out of the desk, smiled, and slipped past him out the door. Her hair smelled like sea water as she went by.

They went down the V.I.P. elevator without speaking, past the numerous security check points and out the back of the building. Her car had been pulled up at the curb. It was low-slung and fast looking, not at all like his little plastic box. It wasn't wired-in like his was either; the driver had complete autonomy and didn't have to log-in to the grid. It gave a low growl as she leapt out into traffic and accelerated.

 **Tacos For Two**

"Where are we going?" Durwood asked.

"It's just around the next corner," she said, slowing to negotiate some major potholes. "Don't they bother to fix the roads any more? I've had to replace the suspension on this thing twice already."

"Maybe you drive too fast."

"Not as fast as I would like." She roared past some little cars chugging along on the grid, startling their gray-faced drivers. She turned right at the next corner and swooped into a parking lot next to a cinder block building. There was a sign in front that read: 'Pancho's Upholstery'.

"I don't get it. I thought we were going to eat."

"We are."

"At an upholstery shop?"

"Best Mexican food in town. Irving says the health department doesn't bother him because they think he's some kind of furniture repair guy."

"Who's Irving?"

"Irving Feldman. He's the owner. *El dueño*."

"Right."

It was dark inside. The place was filled with important business types talking too loud and slurping green drinks out of large glasses. They found a place at the back under a huge sombrero nailed to a phony brick wall. A skinny waiter wearing a cowboy hat and cowboy boots took their drink order and disappeared.

She didn't say anything for a long time. She was looking past him, over his shoulder, casually studying the crowd with placid blue eyes, careful blue eyes. Finally she smiled and said, "Well, what do you think?"

"Looks like Irving's got the genuine article here. A little noisy though."

"That's why we came. So we could talk without being overheard."

"So what are we talking about?"

"You. Why you came to see me."

"I was told you could help me find someone."

She smiled again, brighter this time. "Let me guess. The amazing Mr. Quattlebaum. The administration's bete noir. Don't look so uncomfortable. I said we could talk."

The waiter in the cowboy hat suddenly appeared with two margaritas, placed them on the table with cocktail napkins and disappeared.

"Cheers!" she said, and sipped the drink.

"Cheers!" Bob said. "So how can you help me?"

"What do you know about the Q file?"

"Nothing. Never heard of it."

Her laser blue eyes seemed to sharpen and drill tiny holes in him. "They task you with finding Quattlebaum, but don't bother to tell you about the Q file."

"Maybe that's why I was sent to see you."

"Who's your contact on this?"

"I'm not sure I should tell you."

"You're the one that's asking for help. Is Red Tercel in on this?"

Bob sipped the margarita. "He's one of them."

"Do you really know who you are working for?" She was stabbing the margarita with a black straw.

"Well, I assumed it was the President. I talked to him personally. He's the one that sent me to you."

She smiled cryptically and looked away.

He said, "Am I missing something here?"

"Who else have you worked with so far?"

"A guy named Mote."

"Conrad Mote?"

"That's him. You know him?"

"Oh, Jeezus. You *are* in trouble!"

"He's losing ground."

"What ground?"

"With the seniors. He's going to need their votes in the next election, and he's losing it."

"Who told you that?"

"The polls are saying it."

"I thought we rigged all the polls?"

"The one's the public gets, sure. That's the advantage of a 'free market' economy. Everything is for sale. I'm talking about the ones the PAC's and the lobbyists use. They hire their own people. They say his support is eroding with senior citizens."

"That's because the old bastards are dying off. That's what old farts do."

The man looked at his watch impatiently. "Where is that sonovabitch anyway? I thought we were having a meeting."

"Maybe he's getting the wheels on his bed greased."

"We need to think up a new strategy. Something that will restore some of the old excitement."

"You're starting to sound like you are actually worried our boy won't be reelected."

"I am. There's trouble in the air. That bastard Quattlebaum is out there trying to make him look like and asshole. And it's starting to work."

"So what? He is an asshole. American voters love

assholes. They filled Congress to the brim with them. That's because they are even dumber assholes themselves. To a bunch of imbeciles a mere moron looks like a visionary leader."

"Yeah, but there's another faction at work that wants to replace him and may steal his thunder if we don't do something about it."

"Well, if you're really worried maybe we could crank up the war on terror again. Scaring the hell out of people with terrorists is always a sure winner."

"True. But there is something else out there on the horizon too. A potentially embarrassing report from one of our agencies is missing. If it gets into the wrong hands . . ."

El Supremo suddenly burst through the door, surrounded by black-helmeted attendants pushing his bed. He was followed by a train of fat guys in motorized wheelchairs wearing gray suits and worried looks. They bumped chairs crowding each other, jockeying for position next to their chief. It was the notorious Inner Circle.

"You guys, out!" El Supremo said, indicating the helmet-heads. They shuffled outside obediently, shut the door, and stationed themselves in the hallway.

El Supremo's bed made a whirring sound as he motored to the head of the conference table. He looked around irritably at the expectant group. "Okay, let's get started. Take a seat, everyone.Yuk! Yuk!...Tony, you're the fucking press secretary. How come I'm not getting my name in the news as often?"

Tony Glickman shrugged. He had a smooth round face, placid brown eyes and a bald head. "I'm giving out more press releases than ever. I'm giving a briefing every day. In fact I have another one downstairs in about fifteen minutes."

"Then what's the problem?"

There was a painful silence, then Belcher, his campaign manager, spoke up. "People are getting bored. None of the stories have legs."

El Supremo elevated the back of his bed a few inches and looked at him sharply. "Bored? What are you trying to say, Belcher?"

"Just that the public has a short attention span. You know that. They want more action. More drama. They need something they can sink their teeth into and get excited or pissed off about."

El Supremo frowned. His eyebrows went up and down. "More drama, eh?" He swiveled his head around. "What do you think, Pinky?"

Freddy Pinkman, a political strategist who had honed his skills in rough and tumble Chicago politics, nodded. "He's got a point. I think we need to look more dynamic. Kick ass. A commander-in-chief actually commanding something, instead of just nagging those incompetent pussies in Congress."

"You saying we need a crisis of some kind?"

"We need something. A crisis is good. A disaster of some kind would be even better. Disasters are always good as long as they can be blamed on someone or something else. The president always gets a lot of press during a disaster."

Tony spoke up, "But we can't just wait around until

some disaster to strike."

Belcher turned in his seat and raised one eyebrow slightly. "Well, that's exactly the point, isn't it?"

Tony looked doubtful. "Well, I'm not sure. But then I'm just the press secretary, not a strategist. In any case, I've got a briefing to give. I'm sure you gentlemen will think of something. Mr. President. Gentlemen." He took his attaché case from next to his chair, nodded to the men around the table and rolled towards the door, leaving Belcher's statement still hanging in the air.

El Supremo let rip a huge fart as the door shut. He turned to Belcher. "I know what you're suggesting, but can we do something like that, something dramatic, without having our fingerprints all over it?"

"Absolutely," Belcher said confidently. "It's just a matter of having the right plan and hiring the right people."

"That's what I mean. Hiring the right people is always a fucking problem."

"Not if you know where to look and are willing to pay for their services."

"Money is no problem."

"Sometimes they don't always want money."

"What do they want?"

"You never know. But whatever it is, I'm sure it can be arranged."

"You're an evil, slippery bastard, Belcher. Maybe that's why you've been so successful in Washington. Okay, I'm going to leave it up to you. Just make sure I come out of this looking good."

Pinkman smirked and nodded at the door. "I think

part of the answer to our problem just left."

El Supremo said, "What do you mean, Pinky?" The men around the table looked at Pinkman curiously.

"Simple. The first thing we do to grab some dramatic headlines is charge Tony with espionage. That will get things rolling. Just think, a spy in the very heart of the administration."

There was shock and then excited commentary around the table at the astounding idea. El Supremo chewed on this for a while, working his eyebrows, then nodded slowly. "It's a start … But won't we need something bigger?"

"Absolutely," Pinkman said. "This is just the first act. While all this is going on and you're showing inspiring leadership by smoking out a dangerous traitor we'll figure out a bigger disaster for you to lead us out of."

El Supremo nodded. "Okay, but how do we do it?"

"Simple. We plant some classified material in Tony's house and have the FBI discover it. Have them say it was an ongoing investigation to discover top-secret leaks that were jeopardizing the country's security. It will also send a message to those other assholes working against us. Fuck with us and we'll get you."

Bob Bishop, at the far end of the table, one of El Supremo's more conservative adherents, looked uncomfortable. He finally said in a barely audible voice, "But isn't this kind of unfair to Tony?"

"Fuck Tony." El Supremo snapped. "I never liked that fat little faggot anyway."

Bishop shrugged and sat back in his chair.

Advertising. McCarty was right.

Even in the world of espionage market forces were at work. Information was simply a commodity like everything else, and someone was always willing to provide it if the price was right. Supply and demand. Of course you couldn't take an ad out in the newspapers or on the net in the same way you could with some other item of interest. But there were ways of getting the message out. McCarty had spent his whole adult life negotiating the tangled dimly lit spider webs of intelligence operations, and knew that if you tapped the right strands some interested party would eventually pick up the vibrations. His grizzled and jaded mentor had cautiously put the word out to a select and highly disreputable group of contacts around the world who he knew would pass it on. McCarty loved the game and couldn't keep his hand out, cashiered or not. He had a master painter's eye for subtlety and shades of gray. Maybe it was the moral ambiguity he found so fascinating. He wondered what McCarty had seen in him that had made him decide to take him under his wing. Maybe he wasn't protecting him at all. Maybe he was just saving him for a meal later on.

The Chinese captain blurted something unintelligible over the intercom that L. interpreted as a warning they were about to land. A fat stewardess came down the aisle issuing threats and warnings about the seat backs. He clicked the seat into the upright position and looked out the window.

Far below, the brown and wrinkled Mediterranean was slowly crawling beneath the wing. A parched gray coastline suddenly appeared and melted into the smudged horizon. In a few minutes tumbled clots of raw concrete appeared in the smog and grimy buildings multiplied on the cabin window like a raging infection. A short while later the forlorn, smoggy outskirts of Beirut slipped by, and they were suddenly on the ground.

They marched off the plane under the surly gaze of the flight crew and through the endless labyrinth of partitions and security cameras to the main building. After the usual pointless delays spent in various queues, the passport control agent eyed him suspiciously. He had a shelf of thick eyebrows that formed a solid line across the top of his nose. There was an orange food stain on his shirt. He looked down at the passport, then up at his face to see if the photo matched. He grunted finally and smashed the metal stamper on the document with an emphatic show of force.

Didn't like American apparently. What else was new? No one liked Americans after the global depression that turned wide swaths of the world into hobo camps. Why should these guys be pissed though? What made them think that anyone would want to bail out a bunch of Arabs anyway? Their own leaders wouldn't even help. They just sat on their oil wealth and let things go to hell. He wished it had turned up somewhere else in the world. He didn't like dealing with Arabs or Muslims. They were irrational and dangerously unstable and their politics a study in mass insanity. They were good at making roadside bombs, be-headings, starting murderous riots over cartoons, but not much else. Fuck it. . . Maybe it was just the weather—he didn't always feel that way—maybe it was just all the hoops and the ever increasing misery of air travel.

The heat was intense outside the terminal and he could feel his shirt beginning to soak through. He picked his way among the shouting, jostling crowd that seemed to be on the verge of a riot to where the taxis were lined up like little bright colored beetles.

Rashid was the driver's name. He had a pockmarked face and an irrepressible smile. As they left the airport and fell in line with the other lurching and wheezing bugs. L. wondered if perhaps he was simple minded or had some unfathomable inner secret that allowed him to be perpetually happy. Maybe the fact that he had a job, any job, made him happy, when a third of the planet was unemployed.

The hotel was near the old port, a yellow brick improvisation, next to a two-story pile of blast rubble. An Israeli air strike had taken out the building a couple years before and so far no one had cleared away the debris. A skinny Arab with one empty eye socket checked him in and dropped an old fashioned brass key on the counter in front of him. They still used keys here instead of plastic cards.

A creaking elevator took him up to the third floor and his tiny room overlooking the pile of dusty rubble. He went to the window and looked out. A head bobbed in and out of the light behind a piece of broken concrete. There were people living in the smashed tangle of rubble. He went over to the bed, sat down and flipped open his phone. It was time to make contact with McCarty's man.

The hotel bar was hot, had too many tables, too many flies, and not enough customers. A couple of Arabs in Western business suits sat at a table next to a wheezing air conditioner stuck in the wall. A fuzzy television, hung on chains from the ceiling, reeling off the day's disasters from around the Middle East. An Arab announcer wearing a baseball cap was shouting angrily about something in Jerusalem. L. sat at the bar and waited for the barman to come over. He had a drooping mustache and was twirling a dingy white towel as he watched the news. Occasionally he would snap it with a sharp crack at a fly that had landed somewhere behind the bar. There were several red blotches on the wall.

L. ordered a beer and looked at his watch. Twenty minutes the Fat Man had said. The Fat Man was one of McCarty's contacts, and the two assholes from ops didn't know about him. They would have micro-managed him to death if they had. Cut him out eventually. Fuck the entire operation up even, then blame him for the failure. He sipped his beer and watched the street outside through the dusty windows.

In a few minutes a beat up green taxi pulled up and a skinny guy with wrap around sunglasses got out. He was wearing a white shirt, and carrying an attaché case. He looked up and down the street for a minute, then walked directly into the bar. He glanced at the two Arabs and came over and sat next to L. The barman seemed to know him and brought over a can of Pepsi, then went back to his news and his flies.

The man carefully poured the Pepsi into a glass, and said in a low voice, "You're waiting for the Fat Man?"

L. turned his head to look at him, then looked back out the window. "I'm just a tourist, pal. Don't know any Fat Man."

"Cut the crap, asshole. I'm the Fat Man. McCarty and I go way back. Told me you needed some help. So here I am. Mr. Helpful."

"You look like an Arab pimp. But you talk like a low rent punk from Jersey. You say you're the Fat Man but you don't weigh more that one hundred pounds, sunglasses and all."

"Confusing, isn't it?"

The guy was right, L. thought. He had jumped to a stupid conclusion thinking he had to be fat because of his name in the trade. L. said, "I think we should change bars."

The Fat Man smiled. "The two by the air conditioner? They work for the Chinese. They're off duty now."

"Let's find a new one anyway."

He shrugged, and looked at his watch. "It might be better to wait. But if you insist."

They had only gone a block before L. realized the decision to change bars was a bad one. The Israelis had decided an air strike just then might be fun. Buildings on either side of the street were lifted into the air in huge fiery explosions. Mangled cars were thrown through the front of shops as they disintegrated in the air. Arabs with smoking beards and wild eyes ran past them shouting and crying.

"Stay away from the windows," Fat Man said, looking at his watch. "The concussions can shatter them. I wouldn't want you to get cut."

"Maybe we should look for cover," L. said uneasily.

"Be over in a minute. Three more I think."

Three more explosions in rapid succession slammed the street ahead in gushing volcanos of fire. The jets that had delivered the bombs cleared the city, made climbing turns to the south, disappeared into the haze, and headed back to Israel. That was it for the raid.

L. looked at the Fat Man, walking easily through the smoking debris, carrying his attaché case as if nothing out of the ordinary had happened. "How did you know there would only be three more?"

"The information was available," the man said, giving him a brief smile.

"And you knew when it was going to happen. That's why you said it might be better to wait."

"That too."

"And where do you get this information?"

"All in good time, my friend. All in good time."

They had to pick their way around a broken axle with smoking tires.

"Where are we going, anyway?"

"I know an excellent place. It's just around the next corner."

"How do you know it's still there. Maybe it was hit."

"You needn't worry. It wasn't on the target list. Ah, here we are. We can talk here."

The place was called Abdul's Oasis. They went inside. It had red and green striped fabric hung from the ceiling in an apparent attempt to make it look like a tent. The beige eroding stucco walls had skinny camels and palm trees painted on them. They sat at a table near the windows so they could keep an eye on the fire trucks and emergency vehicles pushing through the streets. They ordered a beer and a Pepsi from a one-armed waiter with a limp.

L. said, "There seem to be a lot of people in this town missing parts."

The Fat Man took his sunglasses off and stared at him for a second with dead fish eyes. "Interesting isn't it?"

"I don't know if interesting is the right word or not."

The Fat Man had taken out a blue handkerchief out and was slowly polishing the lens of his sunglasses. "In this part of the world it is not always easy to make it through life in one piece."

The one-armed waiter carried the drinks over on a tray, sat the tray down on the table, then lifted the glasses off one at a time and took the tray away. They sipped on the drinks and watched the firemen outside move debris to the side of the street.

L. said, "You told me this place would be okay because it wasn't on the target list. How did you know?"

The Fat Man seemed surprised and a little annoyed by his ignorance. "Ahmed over there pays to keep it off. The Israelis use the latest American equipment. When they make a raid to show their power they know exactly what buildings they are going to hit. You can get off the list by paying money. Bombs are expensive so the Jews defray the cost by having the Arab targets pay not to get bombed."

"How do the Israelis collect the money here without getting shot?"

"A middleman, of course. Middlemen are indispensable in this country. Even with God."

L. watched him carefully fold up the handkerchief, tuck it in his coat pocket, and replace the sunglasses on his beak-like nose. L. said, "Okay, sport, when do I get to meet Nasim and pick up my package?"

"It's arranged for tomorrow. You brought the money of course?"

"Of, course."

"In cash?"

"Cold, hard, gringo cash."

Terrorists 'R' Us

He had breakfast at the hotel bar. A Heinekin with a Beck's chaser. At least you could still buy real beer in this part of the world. Back in the land of the free almost everything enjoyable was starting to be banned or taxed so heavily as to be out of reach for most people. A couple of beers first thing in the morning put him in just the right mood for dealing with assholes. Today he figured he would be dealing with a bunch of them.

At exactly twenty past nine he left the bar and walked three blocks south into the old town and the already crowded bazaar. The air was thick with the odor of spices, fish, cooking goat meat and a hundred other unidentifiable smells. He kept checking over his shoulder to see if he had been tailed. No one yet had showed any interest. On a crowded and noisy side street that emptied into the market there was a coffee bar packed to standing room only. His fifty word Arabic vocabulary he had learned on the flight over was good enough to get him a cup of rich black coffee, but no change from the note he put down.

He had almost finished the coffee when someone behind him said, "Would you like to buy a carpet?"

L. turned his head and saw the Fat Man standing next him with a smirk on his face. L. said, "What happened to meeting your sister?"

The Fat Man looked puzzled, "I don't get it."

"Never mind. Take me to your friends."

"They're not my friends. And we do have to buy a carpet. Don't worry though, it will be an excellent souvenir. I'm sure you can put it on your expense account."

The Fat Man led him up the teeming side street then through a series of narrow twisting alleys crowded with tiny shops and shouting, gesticulating Arabs. The treacherous cobblestones underfoot had been worn dark and smooth by hundreds of years of sandaled feet. They went into a shop larger than most with a sign board over the door painted in English: 'Ali's Finest Quality Carpets.'

They were met at the door by a tough looking character who was dressed more like a Chicago bouncer than an Arab. He was jumbo-sized, his face had more scars and pits than a welder's workbench. "What do you guys want?" he said. Definitely American, and none too friendly.

L. turned to the Fat Man, "You sure we got the right place?"

An old Arab with brown burnoose and yellow teeth came over and began talking to the Fat Man in rapid gusts of Arabic. The bouncer edged away and continued looking tough. He was good at looking tough. There was more talk, some money changed hands, then a little more money. Finally the old Arab led them through the shop and around a large pile of brightly colored carpets that nearly reached the ceiling to a heavy wooden door. He unlocked it with two brass keys and pointed them up the stairs with a bony finger. The stairwell was all glazed tile work with intricate patterns. It was lit by a skylight with open sides. They started up the stairs.

• • •

"I thought I was about to get my hands on it then, but when we got to the top of the stairs someone detonated himself in one of the offices. Blew us right back down the stairs. Melted the Fat Man's sunglasses."

"You didn't think it would be that easy did you?" Mc-Carty said, leafing through the file, looking bored.

"I wasn't expecting our source to be located next door to a suicide bomber recruiting and training academy. Must have killed six or seven of the little buggers anyway."

"Happens all the time. Training accident. All low level staffers and rookie instructors probably. I'm sure it didn't take out any of the brain trust."

"Apparently not. The next day they seemed more upset about the busted up computers and furniture than anything else."

"Suicide recruits are a dime a dozen. All the servers that keep their web sites up though are expensive. Seems like they'd keep them away from their operating equipment. The boys must be slipping. Then again the Dubai Brothers always were a little careless. It's a wonder the assholes have survived this long."

"You've met them?"

"Years ago. When I first met the Fat Man. Their real names are Saul and Irving Shapiro. Nice Jewish boys. They started Terrorists 'R' Us right after they graduated from UCLA with degrees in business management."

L. sat up in his chair. "You mean they're Americans?"

"Of course."

"But they spoke with Arabic accents. They have Arab body guards. They've got a picture of Mecca on the wall."

"All for show. It's all marketing. They were the first real businessmen to recognize the untapped profit potential in international terrorism. They saw most terrorists were too parochial in their outlook, were too bogged down by one ideology or another to be really successful. They decided not to let crap like patriotism, nationalism, religion, race or even morality get in the way of making a few shekels. Typical American entrepreneurs you might say. After investing

in a few bribes and some free introductory sample bombings they started a terrorist and intelligence clearing
house open to all comers."

L. rubbed his eyes. "I don't know why I'm surprised.
Anything for a buck."

"Turned out they found a profitable niche. It's terrorists on demand basically. Angry demonstrators with signs
are the cheapest. Rock and bottle throwers and arson-
ists are next. Mobs with Kalashnikovs and jihadists cost
more. Suicide bombers are the most expensive. They sell
to both sides of any conflict and don't discriminate. Need
some stolen nerve gas for a Japanese subway? Look no
further. One stop shopping for disgruntled Arabs, Jews,
Russians, Chechens, Tamils. You name it. If they don't
have it in stock they can usually find it. It's just a question
of money."

"Seems like Mossad or someone would have gotten
pissed at some point. Especially when they're on the re-
ceiving end of it."

"Why would Mossad get pissed? They make a huge
profit on terrorism like everybody else. They even bank-
roll some of the terrorist attacks on Israel. It's a good investment. The more acts of terror in Israel the bigger
their budget gets. The more money their government
asks the U.S. for to fight terror. We give them new planes,
tanks and iron domes. Our factories hire more workers to
make it all. It's a win win situation. Without terrorism, or
the constant threat of terrorism, our economies would be
fucked. Just think how many people the endless 'Threat
of Terrorism' employs. It even employs you."

"Plausible deniability is the overriding concern and must be insured at all stages of any operational initiatives. The mission control officer will report directly to the operations chief of staff all phases of planning, logistics, support and personnel selection for review and authorization." L. was reading from the flimsy yellow cover sheet of a stapled set of documents. McCarty seemed not to be listening, his mind somewhere else.

L. paused and looked up. "Not signed. Just an authorization number. The document was supposed to be destroyed after reading. I wonder why it wasn't"

"Sloppy work." McCarty said tonelessly. He sipped the brandy. "Obviously amateurs were involved once the file was assembled. Amateurs let the file get out."

"It doesn't make sense. This shows that all the early terror attacks Quattlebaum is wanted for the NSA planned and carried out themselves. I can't believe it!"

"Your government at work."

"He was basically a nobody to begin with, just another average citizen. Turned out he was a natural, and dangerous, once they framed him and he decided to live the part. But what was to be gained by making him into this huge international bogeyman?"

McCarty sighed wearily. Oh, don't be so naive. He was scapegoat for something. More power was the initial goal. The bigger the threat, the more power you demand,

and the bigger the budget, just like the Israelis, who play us like a violin. The goal of the agency is not to thwart terrorism, it's to thwart its enemies. That's its first priority. The second one is to cover its ass. Someone screwed up. The people who researched and compiled the Q file actually did an objective analysis. Not all the department heads knew, or would have approved.

"There are competing factions involved. The facts were all true. That was the problem. The contents are a huge embarrassment to the mutants currently in control of the administration. If there's one thing that's dangerous for a government it's the truth. To govern effectively you have to swindle people. These morons obviously didn't get it. At some point they were mismanaged. Worse, some parts of the file were leaked before they could be quashed."

"I guess that makes us both suckers, eh, McCarty?"

"Everybody's a sucker for something. Right now though, you've got a problem. That file can burn a lot of people if it gets in the wrong hands, you included."

"I'm just the lowly messenger boy."

"Bearing bad news for your handlers."

"I haven't told them I have it yet."

"They already know."

The Plumbers

"I've got a little assignment. A freelance job. I need some back-up. The pay is generous enough to make me think it's important to someone. Want to go with me?"

"What's it about?"

"A chance to practice your tradecraft. A little B & E. No rough stuff. In and out in a couple minutes. All very clean. Low risk."

"What's it for?"

"That would be telling."

"Got to worry about coming down on the wrong side of something. You taught me that."

"Smart boy. Don't worry. I wouldn't jeopardize your best interests. I can tell you it's for a good cause in the long run."

"What about the short run?"

"Things always look confusing in the short run."

"Sure it's not a set-up of some kind?"

"Of course it's a set-up. That's why I agreed to it."

"So what's up your sleeve if you agreed to it?"

"That's where you come in."

"Wait a minute now. . ."

"I'm afraid I'm going to need some of those important documents you retrieved."

"Oh, no. I went to too much trouble to get them."

"With my help. I'll only need the file a minute."

"To make a copy. It's my neck if they find out."

"As it stands right now, it's your neck anyway."

The latest intelligence assessments all said the same thing. No sign of Quattlebaum in more than six months now, an unusually long time between sightings by the countless intelligence agencies and their pervasive network of informants. Something big was feared, some extravagant show of defiance that would embarrass the government and El Supremo personally. That had always been the pattern in the past.

The heads of the agencies were frantic. Important jobs were at stake; well-paid heads would roll. Worse, publicity of Quattlebaum's legitimate exploits was getting harder and harder to keep from the masses even though they were used to being spoon-fed crap everyday and accepted the most outrageous lies as gospel. Controlling the lapdog press was no problem of course, their dedication to the entrenched oligarchy was long-standing and absolute. They were as much a part of the established power structure as any big business. They would have no truck with real news if it wasn't in their best corporate interest. And the administration knew exactly which buttons to push to show them it wasn't. It was the rumor mongers and the fringe elements that were doing all the damage. Quattlebaum might just kindle a latent subversive spark that could prove difficult to stamp out if the citizenry ever decided to wake up.

"No more stunts like the Enterprise," El Supremo

had demanded, ending the interview with a long string of obscenities and a series of crazy-eights on his surprisingly agile Lay-Z-Dude bed.

The "Big E" file was nearly two feet thick all by itself. Bob had to admit the idea of one man sinking a nuclear powered aircraft carrier did have a certain flair to it, even though it was a military disgrace, a budgetary disaster, and an act of high treason. Sinking it in San Diego harbor so no one was drowned was a criminal feat of imagination and daring without parallel. Damage control had worked overtime on that one (the boat was being partially submerged for testing). But still there were embarrassing rumors circulating.

All news to Durwood. He was becoming a little alarmed at his own naiveté. There was a strange unknown world outside the comfortable one he knew, the safe, well protected one he saw portrayed on television every night. Sure, he watched all the intellectual shows, all the current affairs with in-depth analysis by witty ex-weathermen, giggling news-anchor women in the morning, kept up on the numerous polls, the self-improvement channels, all the right viewing choices. But apparently it wasn't enough. He was still missing something. He decided to make a big pot of coffee-close.

"Corvetta," he yelled into the bedroom where three wall televisions were droning away. "You hear any rumors last year about one of our aircraft carriers sinking?"

"Everybody heard about it . . . *Duh!*"

"I didn't."

"You don't read the blogs. Besides, you're an attorney."

He took a sip of imitation coffee. ". . . So?"

"So . . . How smart could you actually be?"

It was dark and starting to rain. The sidewalks began to glass over and reflect the street lights in shimmering puddles. L. didn't change his pace as he crossed the intersection and turned left in front of a vacant shoe store with a dingy 'For Lease' sign in the window. Ahead, a car waited at the curb in the shadows. As he approached, the right turn signal blinked once. L. turned, looked back the way he came. No sign of a tail. He stood there for a second, then pulled the door open and climbed in.

"Nasty weather," McCarty said enthusiastically. McCarty wore a black windbreaker and a Detroit Tigers baseball cap. The car smelled damp and musty.

"Why are you so fucking cheerful?" L. said.

"I thought you wanted to be a spy. This is perfect weather for spies. Very atmospheric. Rainy, foggy. Just like in the old movies."

"The rain didn't pick up sulfuric acid and airborne fecal matter on its way down in those days."

"The price of progress, my boy. You sound like one of those old discredited liberal queens who wanted to regulate industry and protect the environment. Where would we be then?"

"Maybe someplace we could at least breathe."

McCarty laughed and started the car. The wipers made a sucking sound as they sqeegeed water off the windows. "Just wait until we get those neck meters. You'll look upon this as the golden age."

"Where are we headed?"

"Not far. Cheney Chase."

"How do you know he won't be home?"

"He's at the Press Club this evening. Passing out the party line, what goes for news these days."

L. didn't say anything and tried to adjust the tiny seat. It only moved a couple inches. "Where did you get this smelly piece of crap?"

"Requisitioned it—as it were—from someone in your section. Just for tonight though."

"Won't they miss it?"

"Not before it's too late. Off on assignment somewhere. Belize, I think. Your people are terrible at keeping secrets."

"Probably in the wrong business. Like me."

McCarty glanced at him. Rain pelted the roof and hood as they splashed through the pot-holed streets. Yellow lights blinked in front of some of the major chasms.

"The infrastructure is rapidly collapsing." McCarty said. "When a country's roads go the end can't be too far behind."

They picked up speed as they left the Inner Grid and headed south over the river. McCarty inserted a plug into a port next to the onboard computer. He plugged the other end into a small black device with a keypad and a tiny screen.

"Time to override traffic control." McCarty explained. L had seen the device before. It not only released them from traffic control undetected, but logged in phony location information that couldn't be traced later.

McCarty took control as the autopilot disengaged with a lurch. They drove in silence. The rain started to let up as they turned off the interstate and into the suburbs. McCarty checked the nav screen. He said, "Hand me that bag in the back seat."

L. twisted around, found a canvas bag in back of McCarty and brought it up front and placed it between the seats. They drove another couple miles. The roads were better here, wider, with fewer potholes. The houses behind tall concrete walls with artificial landscaping looked more substantial, better cared for. A large lighted sign with cursive gold letter letters announced Cheny Chase next right. It was a gated community like the rest.

"Should be a gate house about a hundred yards from the corner," McCarty said, checking the mirrors. "Good so far. No traffic in either direction."

The gate house was a white octagonal with lots of phony gingerbread molding and a tall white iron double gate behind. They coasted up to the large brightly lit window and stopped. It was like looking into an aquarium. The guard inside had his back to the window and was eating a sandwich, watching television on a small screen.

McCarty reached inside the bag and was out the door in one swift, silent movement. He glided over to the door next to the wall and pointed at L. L. slid over to the driver seat and tapped the horn. The guard swiveled in his chair and looked annoyed. It took him a while to get up, put his sandwich down, take a sip of soda, and shuffle to the door. He stuck his head outside to shout something when McCarty tasered him from behind. He went down immediately, a mass of twitching and gurgling. McCarty dragged him by the collar into the gate house. He had him trussed up in tie-wraps by the time L. came in. McCarty took a ring of keys from the man's belt loop and dragged him into a storage closet and propped his head up on some cartons of cola. He took a roll of silver duct tape out of his pocket, peeled off a section and slapped it over the man's mouth. "Take his hat. Keep your face hidden in one of those magazines on the desk. Open the gate for everyone that drives up. You don't want to have to talk to them first. Watch the monitors and keep me posted on the patrols. There should be four of them."

"How does the gate work?"

"On the console there. Green opens." He hit the green button. "Red shuts. Keep him in the closet. Use more tape if you have to." McCarty ducked out of the gate house and back into the car. He was through the gate before it was all the way open.

L. put the guard's hat on, pressed the red button and sat down to wait. There was a bank of two dozen tiny monitors on the wall that constantly cycled though the estate. He could see McCarty's car moving slowly down one of the lanes. Nothing else was moving on the watery roadways.

McCarty drove slowly, following the GPS voice directions. The houses were all New Age mansions. Lots of pointless Disneyland facades, faux grandeur. They looked as impermanent as a movie set. "Security patrol running parallel to you next block south," he heard L. say through his headset.

"Roger, Quarterback."

The rain had started to come down hard again through the night sky, turning the streets into long black mirrors. He stopped at the next corner, turned the car off and waited. He could see the glare of approaching headlights off the slick curbstones on the next corner down. He couldn't see the whole intersection, but he could see the rain caught in the lights. The lights held steady in the silvery curtain of rain, as though the other driver had paused too. McCarty doubted he had a scanner sophisticated enough to pick him up. Besides, he had disabled the transponder in the car and had installed an electronic chaff device. It was perfect for this weather.

At last the lights swung away to the right and lost intensity. He started the car again and nosed out into the intersection. The lights were now just two tiny red smears in the distance. He left his lights off and drifted silently as a shadow through the empty streets. There were only a few lights on in the lonely looking houses that seemed to shiver in the rain. The rich went to bed early here,

McCarty observed. Without his lights the rain made it hard to read the streets signs. The GPS voice instructions told him it was the next street though: Ladrones Lane. He turned right then went into a long curved brick driveway that ended in an iron gate supported by two masonry pillars. A concrete wall surrounded the grounds. He would be on several cameras now. Electronic security would be monitoring his every move from five different angles.

It was time to go to work.

"Quarterback, give me an update," he said opening the car door.

"Nothing here. Two units parked window to window. Looks like they're bullshitting and eating donuts."

"Okay. Get ready. Some alarms are going to go off soon."

L. found him on one of the little monitors that lined the room on three sides. He was working at something on one of the pillars that supported the gate, breaching the electronic security with the cool, unhurried efficiency of a professional thief. A red warning light started blinking on the console, accompanied by an intermittent buzzing. L. leaned over, switched it off and looked back at the screen. McCarty was already on the top of the wall. In another second he had dropped over the side. He was inside the grounds now. L. scanned the monitors. The two patrol units were still window to window. There was nothing for him to do now but wait. He looked at his watch. Four and a half minutes McCarty had said, once he was inside the wall.

Another red light came on, and an insistent buzzing.

He got up from the desk and went to the storage room door and opened it a few inches. The guard was still on the floor, tied up. He stopped struggling against the tie-wraps and looked at L. with wide eyes. A muffled, angry sound came through the duct tape wrapping his lower face.

L. said, "Calm down, Barney. We'll be gone in a few minutes. Oh, by the way, that was a pretty good sandwich. I prefer the deli mustard though." He closed the door and went back to the desk to wait.

A car turned off the highway by the entrance and came down the driveway towards the gate house. L watched it as it approached. It was a silver Hangchow saloon with six headlights. A geezer car. Geezers needed a lot of lights to drive at night. An old man with a white pinched face was driving. There was a young blonde next to him on the front seat. L., his face partially hidden behind a sports magazine, gave him a lazy wave and hit the gate button. The old man, L. knew, wouldn't be thinking about him, or notice anything out of place. He was obviously thinking about getting a piece of ass. People so occupied don't usually notice a whole lot around them.

L. looked at his watch again. Seven minutes now. Jesus, what was taking McCarty so long? Another alarm went off. The kill switch didn't work on this one. He scanned the bank of screens. "Oh, oh!" he said. The two patrol units had moved. More lights were blinking now, alarms buzzing. The vid-phone suddenly blinked. It was the local police. Their station was two and a half miles south of the estates. L. hesitated, then put his face right up close to the camera so all they could see was a big nose. "Gate house," he said in a bored voice. A female cop in uniform appeared on the screen.

She said, "Got a buzzer here on thirty-one Ladrones Lane."

"Hang on a minute." He moved out of camera range, pretending to be checking on it, stalling as long as he could. He said, "Nothing here. Had a few false alarms a while back. Happens when it rains. Let me check with some of the road units."

There was a long pause on the other end. She was suspicious now. Finally she said, "We didn't get your nine o'clock report. What happened?"

Was there really a nine o'clock report? Sounded like a trap. Nothing to do but bluff now. "Just a minute. One of our tenants is outside. Looks drunk again. Second time this week. Let me call you right back . . ."

This was cutting it way too fine. The local police would be here in a few minutes now. He opened the exit gate and went outside to stand in the rain. Down inside the estates a vehicle with its lights out was moving in the shadows, approaching through the mist in no apparent hurry. It was McCarty, nonchalant as ever. McCarty stopped and popped the door for him.

L. jumped inside, McCarty released the brakes and started towards the highway.

L. said, "You're late. I was beginning to worry."

"Couldn't be helped."

"Trouble?"

"Not really. Had to kill the dog."

L. gave him a look. "That seems a little drastic for you."

"It was one of those Honda things. A robot. The sucker actually bit me."

A pair of headlights turned in from the highway. L. said, "It's the local cops. I knew it wouldn't be long."

"I'll flag them down."

L. looked at him in disbelief. "I knew this was a mistake."

McCarty slowed, lowered the window and put his arm out. The black and white slowed to a stop next to them and the window came down. A flashlight blinded them and held steady on their faces.

"Turn that damned thing off, Sully," McCarty said.

The man in the car snapped the light off and laughed. "McCarty, you bastard, up to your old tricks again."

"And some new ones too. Just don't give up any of the evidence without a thorough inventory and description."

"Don't worry, Mac. I don't like those assholes any better than you do. You better move it though." He rolled up the window, turned on his flashing lights and disappeared through the exit gate they had left open. A half-mile after McCarty had turned right on to the highway three more police cars passed them going in the opposite direction and turned in at the driveway.

L. studied him for a minute, then said, "Okay, lets have it. Who else is in on this little caper I don't know about?"

McCarty answered him easily without taking his eyes off the road. "Relax. No one important. It's just the effabee-eye. They're being used like everybody else. They're scheduled to raid the place tomorrow morning and find the so-called evidence. The break-in was supposed to go undetected. But somehow I bungled that."

"On purpose. But why?"

"So the police will have all the evidence and the FBI will have to officially pull rank to take it away from them. And what I planted was the wrong stuff."

"You substituted the Q file everyone's afraid of."

"They want to frame this guy as a spy for some reason. Don't know why exactly. The President's wheelchair buddies probably needed a fall guy for one of their hare brained schemes. They try to sacrifice the poor slob now, the classified material they find in his house won't be the garden variety secrets. It'll be the toxic Q file."

"So if they try to prosecute him the contents of the file may become public."

"That's the general idea."

"Nice little double cross. I'm beginning to think you may have some buried scruples after all."

"I'll probably get over it."

"Won't this cause some problems for you with the

people who paid for this little exercise?"

"I'm not too worried. Cowardly amateurs with no loyalties to anything but their own self-interests."

"They could still retaliate."

McCarty shot him a look and grinned. "Well, there's more than just the Q file out there. You might say there's a whole alphabet waiting to be discovered."

"Your ace in the hole."

"A deck of aces. Should have never fired me."

Back To The Mine

Bob decided to go over the early stuff on Quattlebaum. He didn't really know what he was looking for, but he guessed that's where the clues to what made him really tick would be.

Quattlebaum first came to the attention of the state in kindergarten. "An uncooperative subject," Mrs. Tutweiler reported, "unwilling or unable to assimilate standard socialization methods. Hostile. Combative. Refused on numerous occasions mandatory relaxants and urine tests for illegal drugs. Tests administered forcibly 9/28."

Always on the lookout for dangerous subversives, Mrs. Tutweiler added a supplement: "Parents seem to lack proper sympathy for the state in this matter. Recommend thorough background checks and possible intervention and custody of subject by appropriate agencies."

Curiously, the background checks were missing. Custody records gone too. Durwood thought about this for a moment, wondering if it was important. He got up to make another pot of coffee-close.

 Gambit Offered

It was just starting to get light when the vid-phone buzzed. Durwood rubbed his eyes wearily and punched the button on the wall. His hello came out mostly as a yawn.

"Durwood?" The voice on the other end was mechanical, synthesized, and the view screen was blocked so he couldn't see the caller's face. "Red Tercel here. How's it going?"

He hesitated, wondering what Tercel's connection was with this. "Er... fine."

"Don't be coy, Durwood ... We're in this together. I'm working on the same thing you are. You need to understand El Supremo's methods a little better if you're going to get anywhere around here. He always gives the same job to more than one person. That way he doesn't have to depend on any one individual. You can probably see why after Mote's little desert fiasco ... Anyway, what I had in mind was a little strategic cooperation. You help me, I help you. That way we both prosper."

"I don't know."

"Look, Quattlebaum is an enemy of the state. A big problem for El Supremo. If we don't get rid of his problem, he'll get rid of us, and find someone who can. End of career for promising young attorney ... Now what have you come up with so far?"

Durwood had to think it over. It could be just a bluff. On the other hand, Tercel could be a dangerous enemy.

"Nothing much, except most of the standard reports are worthless. The analysis all reads like hack work from staff, simple minded or totally incompetent."

"Well, at least you got that right. Have you read any of the Burdley documents?"

"Not yet. Everyone says he's a crank. Dismissed as unreliable."

"I'm not so sure ... Look them over. Maybe there's something there. I'm working on it from a different angle, trying to track down his former friends. I'll get back with you soon and give you an update." He switched off.

"Hmm... Maybe... Maybe not," Durwood said thoughtfully, staring at the blank screen.

More Dirty Deeds

He put the thick file back in its plastic case and replaced it in the box. He could see in the footnotes and references cited the disturbing outline of a mountain of reports, a wilderness of investigations, studies and countless other documents bulging in the secret archives of the bureaucracy. How many agencies, sub-agencies, offices and task forces were involved in this anyway? What he was looking at now was merely the summaries of some of those reports.

All in all, there was very little solid information to show for it. The after-the-fact analysis led nowhere and everywhere at the same time. Platitudes of culpability. Lax security, poor training, inter-service rivalry, gross negligence incompetent officers. Useless hack work. None of it very substantial, or very helpful.

Each of the huge blue files marked with Top-Secret tabs proved to be similar calculated assaults on El Supremo's prestige:

Intelligence Agency Document BD512/16QB:
Report on the Theft and Destruction of the Presidential Craftmatic Bed

National Security Report 577Q/99TR
The Atlanta Attack on the President's Motorcade by Trained Rodents

Air Force Intelligence Document AF-ZIG 99878/69Q
Summary Report on the Theft of "Ziggy," the President's Parrot

And so on.

•••

The Section Chief adjusted the blinds fractionally on the window next to his desk, then sat down heavily. "Go on," he said.

"She assumed there were no bugs or any surveillance, so she was fairly unguarded in her comments."

"We will study the written report in detail later. Just give us the highlights for now."

"Well, as you know, we have a growing file on Morganfliess. As more resources became available to our section we've been able to expand our scope of research and information collection on more potentially important subjects. This Durwood has recently been added to our files as well due to his recent assignment of responsibilities by a faction in the administration."

"He's not working for NSA then?"

"Uncertain. At least, he wasn't initially."

"Who's his control?"

"It's at the top. Tercel, apparently."

The Section Chief frowned. "This is not good news. Another eager and naive amateur with a law degree and a hunting license from those bunglers at the top. Not good at all."

"It is a problem, sir. And he seems to be very dilligent, or at least highly active, in his snooping efforts."

"Dammit, if there's one thing I hate it's a government employee who takes his job seriously."

"Maybe it's not surprising, really. He's young. He's digested too many of those soppy platitudes they still teach in school about achieving success. God knows why."

"Amateurs! Hasn't he realized yet that efficiency and

productivity are the mortal enemies of bureaucracy. Does he know about the Q file?"

"He does now."

"That damn file is going to get us all hung if the wrong people get their hands on it. The Inner Circle is scrambling already. The next election has them worried."

"I've heard something is up. Some kind of preliminary effort."

"I wonder who they will tap for the dirty work?"

"Maybe the Israelis. They're hiring a lot out outside contractors and freelancers now."

"I should have retired when I had a chance. This business has gone to hell."

"You want to finish this later?"

"No. Give it to me now. I wish these damn hemorrhoids would quit acting up. What else have you got?"

"Durwood and Morganfliess may be having an affair."

Body Heat

It took a long time to develop. As their professional lives became more intertwined their personal relationship began to change imperceptibly. Morganfliess was aloof and totally professional the first month he worked with her. While he sifted through cases of documents and endless reports looking for a lead occasionally she would condescend to offer a clue that would point him in another direction. She seemed to mock his ignorance and naiveté regarding the labyrinthine world of intelligence gathering that she had grown up in. Insensibly her attitude changed and she seemed to be more amused than exasperated by his innocence. They began to meet more regularly, and at later hours, to discuss strategy and formulate plans. Her apartment and the surrounding restaurants became familiar to him. He discovered she was an excellent cook, something that Corvetta never was. She eventually dropped her pretense of indifference, and not much later, her dress, along with her inhibitions. Bob was swept away by a creature of dazzling beauty, superior intelligence and demanding appetites. His home life seemed even more desolate and uninviting than it was before. Corvetta, with the faultless radar and territorial instincts wives invariably possess, sensed something was amiss. She watched with patience and disgust his growing distance and contemplated her response.

"Is he insured?" asked Emily, her rammer girlfriend from upstairs. Emily had been her closest friend and confidant since they discovered they both hated exactly the same people in the building, which was nearly everyone they were acquainted with.

"Yeah, he's got great insurance. The government gives its people the best."

"Then let me ram the little fucker for you. I'll smash him like a bug. We just stick a locator on that piece of shit he drives, when he's driving home from work I'll pick up his signal, and … Bam! Like a insect on the windshield. End of story. Money in the bank."

"Wouldn't it be dangerous?"

"Naw. Accidents happen all the time on the corridor. Cars break down constantly. It's our job to blast them into pulp so things keep moving. Remember that old Jewish bag that lives next to the trash shoot on my floor, always whining, complaining, nagging me to turn my music down, always bitching about something?"

"Mrs. Gonzalez with the red hair?"

"Yeah, that's her."

"I didn't think she was a Jew."

"She acted like one." Emily winked significantly. "Anyway, she had one last week. A major mishap. Probably on the way home from an early bird special somewhere. Didn't know what hit her. Sluiced off my rig and now she's history. Didn't even leave a dent."

"Didn't they investigate?"

"Not seriously. Lack of funds. Probably all they found was a stolen set of salt and pepper shakers, knowing her."

Corvetta considered a minute, touched by her friend's kindness. "Wow!... You would do that for me?"

Emily was picking the scab off her latest tattoo, a swastika made out of red roses. "Sure, baby. I never liked that little wanker anyway... Hey, you never did show me your new boobs."

The buildings drifted by like silent ghosts in the green-ish smog as the tiny plastic car followed the computer coordinates Durwood had punched in an hour earlier. He had never been to this end of the great, sprawling city be-fore. The subcultures out this way had been dangerous at one time, noted for their violence and their music before they had been subdued, pacified by the great Social Uni-formity Campaigns.

"Approaching coordinates," the panel speaker an-nounced. "Further instructions please."

"Disengage," Durwood ordered. "I'll take it from here."

"Negative. Sensors indicate driver fatigue and stress. New coordinates, please."

"I said disengage. I'm not tired."

"Negative. Violation of Uniform Traffic Code. For your protection, attempts to circumvent this this sys-tem are punishable by not more that seven years in jail and fines of not more than fifty thousand credits. This warning can be used against you in court. Thank you for your cooperation."

The car decelerated and pulled into the right lane, flashing its lights as it slowed, seeking a police monitor station to log onto.

He decided to take a chance and unplug the control unit anyway. This was for El Supremo and for national security. Sometimes you needed to bend the laws in order to save them. He got rid of the flashing lights by kicking loose the black box under the dash and ripping off the dangling wires. The car bucked and lurched as he regained control and swerved on to the exit ramp. He began looking for street signs in the vaporous light.

Burdley's narrow street was in a sluggish backwater of the city composed mostly of warehouses and the gloomy remains of factories from the industrial era. The faces he saw on the other side of the windshield looked pinched and gray, expressionless, with hollow eyes that looked right through him. It could have been a city of sleepwalkers. He parked the car next to a huge dumpster.

Hooked On Books

'Burdley's Bookstore,' a dim liquid crystal sign announced just above the entrance. The hinges protested loudly as he pushed the door open. It was dark and musty inside and no one seemed to be around.

The ancient books, in all shapes, sizes and colors, were piled nearly to the ceiling, overflowed the shelves and spilled on to the floor. Not much market for these Durwood supposed, not since everything of any value had long since been transferred to electronic media. These were the marginal leftovers, the dry husks of dead ideas, obsolete philosophies and antiquated systems of thought on one last stop before they turned to dust and disappeared into oblivion.

He took a second to scan some of the shelves. The titles were arcane and curious. Ancient, obscure authors all too irrelevant to be remembered. He read some of the strange sounding names aloud: "Cervantes, Pushkin, Shelly." He recognized none of the names or titles.

A voice close to his ear startled him. "I have the complete works of T. S. Eliot if you're interested."

He turned and was confronted by a pair of thick glasses and a shock of nearly white hair.

"Never heard of him."

"Your education has been sorely neglected then."

"I have an excellent education."

The man smiled. "Perhaps in some small circles."

"And in some circles they think Ian Burdley is a hopeless crackpot in need of state supervision."

Burdley studied him for a moment through the thick lenses. He was at least a head taller than Durwood. "I can see you are not a bibliophile as I first thought. Obviously you are here on another mission."

"I came to talk to you about Morton Quattlebaum."

Burdley frowned. "I see. I should have guessed from the cut of the clothes. Another ambitious company man. But what good would the information of a crackpot be?"

"I didn't say you were a crackpot. Just that some people thought so. I was hoping you could help me."

Burdley regarded him doubtfully, then reluctantly led him through the maze of precarious shelves to a windowless office in back. "We can talk in here. Have a seat."

Durwood sat down on a rickety red plastic chair. He said, "Burdley, I really do need your help. I'm looking for some clue. Some piece of information. . . I don't know what exactly. I need to know what makes him tick."

Burdley leaned back in his chair, put his feet up on the desk and laughed. "Look—What did you say your name was?"

"Durwood."

"Look, Durwood, forget it. The studies I did for the CIA, the NSA and all their many cohorts have long since been discounted. They didn't take me seriously from the beginning. I recommend you go back home and try a little TV for a while, or whatever you bureaucrats do for a good time. Can't bruise your career as easy that way."

Durwood looked around at the ancient furniture, the obsolete office machinery. It almost looked like a stage set. "You know, I wondered what I would find when I got here, Burdley. You're kind of a disappointment really. You should have known the agencies are filled with incompetents, with a bunch of dull-witted yes-men protecting their own turf. So they rejected all your ideas and passed on your recommendations? You resigned and now where are you? A junk dealer walking around in cobwebs. If you help me out there's a chance for revenge, redemption."

Burdley didn't say anything for a full minute, scratching his chin thoughtfully. "Well, you may be right. ... But I still say forget it. My information couldn't do you any good. Quattlebaum certainly didn't help my career. What makes you think you'd do any better listening to me?"

"No reason in the world. Maybe your ideas are all

whacko. But if it's any consolation, none of the other analyses have produced anything but failures. Quattlebaum is
still at large."

"And likely to remain so. He seems to have the uncanny
ability to outguess you people at every turn."

"So what is it, Burdley? How do you get to be Morton
Quattlebaum? What turns someone into a terrorist and
drives him year after year?"

"Assholes like you."

Durwood heard Burdley could be difficult, irascible,
possibly a little unbalanced. He would let it slide.

"No offense intended," Burdley continued. "But I'm
afraid that is what Quattlebaum's assessment would be.
He has a deep-seated hostility towards people like you."

"What have I ever done to him?"

"You don't know his real history. He sees you as part of
a implacable, mindless machine that will go to any lengths,
that will stop at nothing to destroy him."

"What does he expect? He doesn't obey the laws. He's
a criminal."

"The founders of this country were criminals. They
didn't obey British laws. He sees himself cut out of the
same cloth. He's operating on a completely different set
of principles. He's not just another criminal out for personal gain. There's a consistent logic to his actions if you
can divorce yourself from the standard assumptions most
people operate under."

"Such as?"

"He doesn't believe he's the possession of the state. He
doesn't believe the state has the right to intrude into every

aspect of his personal life. That you have the right to some secrets from the state. Antique ideas essentially, ones that have been completely discarded over time, replaced by what we now accept without question."

"C'mon, Burdlley, this is the freest country in the world. The country protects him from the cradle to the grave, solves all his problems—"

"Where you're only free if you agree. A government, he would point out, that is highly privileged and permanently entrenched. That increasingly limits his freedom, searches his urine, invades his privacy while claiming to protect his liberty. That manipulates the press to portray acts of tyranny as protecting people's rights. A government now almost totally given over to the methods of a police state while busy applauding itself for its freedoms and democratic traditions."

"These your opinions too, Burdley?"

"Don't forget I tried to catch him like everybody else. Of course they wouldn't listen. My ideas were too outlandish, too bizarre."

"Okay, okay, Burdley. Let's say you're right. The guy's totally fucked with all these weird ideas. Whacked to the max. Still, there's got to be some kind of angle in all this. Something we can use to set him up. A hook we can use to lure him in."

Burdley thought it over a while. "What's in it for me?"

"As I said, vindication perhaps. Rehabilitation. You can come out of hiding and be the baddest fish in the think tanks again."

"No thanks."

"A lot of rewards will come down if we score."

"Like maybe no neck meter for a while, as they're planning for most of our citizens?"

"Probably. At least plenty of free time at a minimum."

"You want me to help you build a trap."

"Exactly. You've had a good long time to think it over, and rethink it probably. What can we use to build it around?"

"Hmmm. . ." Burdley scratched his chin thoughtfully. Bob was right apparently, the idea had crossed his mind before. Burdley stared at the ceiling for a long time, then finally said, "First, assuming I did agree to help you, it would have to be something subtle... More than subtle—diabolical. Like a chess stratagem seven moves deep. Based on something trivial, routinely overlooked in all the background reports, apparently meaningless, but if used properly, ultimately fatal."

"Now you've got it."

"Something so cunning, devious and unexpected that even the wary Quattlebaum won't perceive it."

"Exactly."

Burdley leaned across the desk and smiled at him. His eyes behind the glasses were as big as light bulbs. "Actually, it's quite simple, Bob."

"What is it?"

"A tiny bread crumb trail. Something he wouldn't dream could have any significance at all."

"What?"

Burdley sighed, and shook his head. "No. You probably wouldn't believe it. You're just like the others."

"Tell me, Burdley! What the hell is it?"

Burdley stared at him for a long time without speaking, then finally smiled and said, "Pizza."

Gambit Accepted

Durwood looked at him incredulously. "Pizza?"

"Absolutely. With anchovies... And beer... Real beer, of course. He loves beer."

Bob grunted, then stood up and smiled scornfully. "Okay, okay. I guess they were right, Burdley. Maybe you are a lunatic after all. And you decided to string me along for a laugh... Well, congratulations. You got a little revenge... See ya around, old timer." He turned for the door.

"I'm serious. Think it over a second, Durwood. It sounds crazy, and it may be. But it is a weakness, and a weakness can be exploited if you have imagination and think outside the lines. He's addicted to pizzas with anchovies, and loves beer. It's buried there in one of the personality profiles. I'm sure you've come across it. Now just think, with the massive computer resources you have at hand, combined with the readouts of all the air monitoring devices your friends have just installed, you can analyze the air of every building in the country, locate at any particular time anyone eating pizzas with anchovies and drinking real beer. The fumes of such a pungent combination are unmistakable. Italian intelligence has done extensive research on the matter."

"There must be thousands of people eating pizza and drinking beer at any one time."

"Not that own a parrot."

"A parrot? What's a parrot got to do with all this?"

"He owns a parrot that likes pizza. El Supremo's parrot, in fact, Ziggy. He stole it from him. You must have read the report. They're inseparable now. Another reason why he hates Quattlebaum."

"So what?"

"So you analyze those batches for parrot farts."

"Parrot farts?"

"Absolutely. Parrot farts are quite unmistakable chemically. They have a unique signature that could be easily identified with the right software."

Bob didn't know whether to believe him or not. Was he just putting him on or was there something to it? "Hmm . . . It's a weird idea, Burdley."

"No weirder than analyzing urine. The government analyses oceans of it every year for one reason or another. The government routinely checks crotches at the airport, analyzes urine, why not check for parrot farts?"

Durwood frowned, starting to look intrigued by the idea. "You're sure about the parrot farts?"

"Absolutely. I can show you the scientific literature."

"It's a long shot of course. But so far nothing else has worked. You know, you may just have something there," he admitted at last.

Burdley smiled and leaned back in the chair, watching the little wheels turn—reluctantly at first, then with growing momentum.

"It won't be easy," Durwood cautioned.

"The CIA and FBI are used to raw data. Some parrot farts would be right up their alley."

Bob was pacing the floor now. The little hamster was turning the wheel faster and faster. They did have those monstrous Cray computers just idling at the curb. "The cost will be tremendous. We'll have to narrow it down first. At least find out what city he's in at one particular time, then search it block by block, monitor by monitor."

Burdley smiled and said, "I'm sure you'll figure it out. You seem very ambitious. Maybe too ambitious."

Bob stopped pacing, then suddenly thrust his hand out. "Thanks, Burdley. I owe you."

Burdley shook it reluctantly. "You don't owe me anything. Good luck."

Durwood mumbled something about not forgetting him, then was out the door.

Burdley turned to the wall behind the desk and touched the button hidden under the chair moulding. The paneling suddenly parted, revealing a large screen. He swung the keyboard out and leaned back in the chair. He punched at the keys until a grid pattern was brought up.

He removed his glasses and studied it for a minute. Hacking his way into New Detroit's official public safety maps had been relatively easy; accessing its protected directory program had been the hard part. He scrolled the map slowly, watching the veins and arteries of the city unroll. He stopped at the ancient expressway around Inkster, then zoomed to ten square blocks. Luckily, the streets were both short. The transposition of names took only a few seconds. Back to the directory now. It was a little more tricky here because of the double blind encryption and anti-tampering measures. Still, a piece of cake compared to the CIA's little system. Now back to the map for a final check. Everything looked good. The street names were switched. He punched his way out, then sat staring at the blank screen, thinking.

"Let's hope there are no fires for a while," he said. He stood up and pushed the glasses into the wastepaper basket and stood up.

Leaving On A Jet Plane

"Where are they now?"

"Some place called Arty's Fatbuckle."

"What's that?"

"I don't know. Some kind of artsy fartsy coffee house."

"What're they doing there?"

"She dragged him there to listen to poetry."

"Jeezus, why would they want to do that?"

"Who knows?"

"Why is the sound so bad?"

"What do you think? The equipment sucks, as usual. We didn't get a good placement either."

"Turn up the volume."

"It's up all the way ... Listen ..."

"No, it's important....We have to talk about some things, Bob."

"Talk about what?"

"Our relationship, for one."

"What's wrong with our relationship?"

"It's not getting anywhere."

"Why does it have to get anywhere. Why can't it just be?"

"Because I'm unhappy."

"You don't seem like that when we're in bed."

"I want more than a part-time lover. Things seem like they're falling apart. You're still married to that ignorant bitch, Corvetta. And you're mixed up with those degenerate weirdos at the White House."

"Degenerate weirdos? You're talking about the President and his staff. Some of the most important men on the planet. They run this country."

"And they're running it into the ground. The government has turned into something unrecognizable. It's a joke now. It's some kind of deformed monstrosity. An empire of the grotesque."

"I don't know what you are talking about. But you're a part of it too. You're part of the government machinery, Miss Career Intelligence Officer."

"I know, I know. You're right. I went along like everybody else. I guess what I'm saying is that maybe it's time for a change. A big change."

"What kind of change?"

"Getting away from all this. Leave all this depressing crap behind. I know some beautiful spots in South America where people are still relatively sane and they haven't polluted or wrecked everything yet. My father left me with a little money. So we wouldn't have to stay in the same spot all the time. We could travel. See what's left of the world before it totally collapses."

"You mean just up and leave?"

"Why not? Just you and me. It will be a great adventure."

"Leave all this?"

"Leave all what?"

"You're serious, aren't you?

"I'm serious."

"Well. . . okay. But I don't know about leaving. That doesn't sound like getting anywhere. I want to make something of myself. I want to be somebody."

"You already are somebody. Somebody I thought was pretty special. You're Bob Durwood."

"I mean I want to be somebody important. I don't want to be a nobody. Just another *nameless slob living in oblivion, hanging around with a bunch of nameless nobodies, leading a dead-end life like every other cipher."*

"So when you get to be important what are you going to do? Hang out with other important people and talk about how boring unimportant people are?"

"No, that's not what I mean. I mean I just don't want to be like everybody else. I want to be something different. I want people to know who I am."

"Like being the guy who nailed Quattlebaum."

"That would be a start . . ."

(Restaurant noises now. The sound of a chair scraping. Clash of silverware. Background babble of unintelligible conversations.)

"The sound is cutting out again. I can't hear them."

"I think she gave him an ultimatum. She wants him to make a choice between her and his career and ignorant wife."

"Who's that now?"

"The poet they came to listen to. She likes that kind of shit."

"This broad has to be. . ."

"Quiet!. . . Listen. . ."

(More muffled voices. A squeal of audio feedback. A

loud belch, a gust of laughter) Then, barely audible:

> *the little men from fantasyland*
> *have got me on their mind*
>
> *the little men from fantasyland*
> *are watching all the time*
>
> *patrolling in the streets*
> *marching in the halls*
>
> *watching me everywhere*
> *they're listening through the walls*
>
> *the little men from fantasyland*
> *are putting us all in lines*
>
> *they're checking all the time*
> *just checking, so civil and so kind*
>
> *it's very important work you know*
> *. . . keeping me safe from crime*
>
> *from deviates, from infidels*
> *and other forms of slime*
>
> *the little men from fantasyland*
> *are guarding all my rights . . .*
>
> *the little men from fantasyland*
> *have got me in their sights*

(A crash of broken glass somewhere close, one person

clapping weakly, and the sound went dead)

"That's it. The mike crapped out for good."

"Or they found it."

"Maybe. I wish we could've got more. What do you think?"

"I never liked poetry. Only faggots like poetry."

"Not that, you imbecile. I mean about Morganfliess and Durwood."

"They're both crazy. But that don't get us any closer to the Q file."

"Still, the Director is going to be very interested to hear her opinions. It makes her a security risk now."

"I thought everybody was a security risk."

Setting The Locator

Corvetta was creeping down the hall on little cat feet. The building was quiet except for the usual night sounds of machinery starting and stopping somewhere in the huge structure. A couple of the hall lights were out so she had trouble reading the numbers on the doors. A three or an eight? Her face was very close to one of the doors when it suddenly burst open and she was looking into the face of a fat woman with pink plastic curlers. The woman screamed and slammed the door on Corvetta's nose.

Corvetta swore and ran down the hallway. A bar of

light suddenly appeared on the carpet ahead. A door had opened and a woman was leaning out waving her arms. She quickly recognized Emily who waved her into her apartment and shut the door.

"What took you so long?" Emily demanded. She was dressed all in black like a commando.

"I had to wait until Bob was asleep. I wanted to make sure he was really out before I looked for his car keys. Never did find them. Then some old woman nearly scared the shit out of me?"

"Okay. I was wondering what happened to you. We might not even need the keys. I think I might attach it on the outside. I get a stronger signal that way." She put on her assault vest. It was black nylon and seemed to be made mostly of pockets. She ripped open a velcro flap and took out a small plastic box and held it between two fingers to show Corvetta.

"That's a radio?" Corvetta said.

"A locator. A bloodhound 379 XP. GPS synchronized with failsafe redundancy, remotely activated and controlled, with an effective range of 250 miles. Standard FBI, CIA issue. For official use only. Strictly top of the line."

Corvetta looked impressed. "How did you get it?"

"From a Chinese website. A friend in the FBI told me about it. That's where the FBI and CIA buy most of their field equipment. It's a lot cheaper than buying it here. Saves them millions every year."

Emily went into the hall closet and started pulling items off the shelves and stowing them in her assault vest. She handed Corvetta a long black police-style flashlight. "You take this. I've got one but we might need a back up. Take this too." She handed Corvetta a small black canister.

"What is it?"

"Pepper spray. In case we run into some assholes in the garage." She winked, spun Corvetta around by the shoulders and slapped her on the ass. "Okay now, princess. Let's roll!"

They cracked the door first, slipped into the hallway, then quietly shut the door behind them. Emily whispered, "We'll take the stairs. Don't want to use the elevators."

Emily opened the door and led the way down. Their foot steps made small metallic echoes as they wound down the cinder block stairwell. The stairwell lights had been broken out on the underground parking levels. The place smelled like piss. "What level?" Emily asked, snapping on a pen-light to read the number.

"9-D," Corvetta whispered. "God, it stinks in here."

They went down three more levels, Emily leading the way. "This is it," she said, shining her light above the door. She turned the knob and they walked out on to the gray concrete parking garage. It was dimly lit and packed with tiny, silent vehicles. Nothing moved. They had the floor entirely to themselves, a private, lifeless auto museum.

"We're in luck," Emily said. "Not one single asshole. Now where's your spot?"

"Other side, last row. It's next to a column. One hundred ninety-two I think."

Emily looked at her sharply. "You think? Don't you know? We've got to be certain."

"I'll know it when I see it."

"What make?"

"It's a Beijing. One of those Chinese pieces of shit."

"It figures. No wonder you want to get rid of the asshole. No real man buys a Chinese car."

They walked noiselessly down the long, silent rows of little cars looking at the yellow painted floor numbers.

"Here it is," Corvetta said, pointing at one of the little featureless imports. "Bob's econobox. The lowest common denominator personal transportation."

"You're sure? The one next to it is the same make. Almost the same color."

"This is it. One ninety two, just like I said."

Emily shrugged. "Okay, as long as you're certain."

She knelt next to the driver side wheel well, stood the flashlight on end next to the tire and took out the locator. From a pocket in her assault vest she took out two tiny tubes of epoxy cement and activator. She squeezed out a gob of each on the back of the locator, smeared them together, and reached up under the fender. She held it there as it set up.

"I think someone's coming," Corvetta said. There was the sound of tires squealing on the slick concrete on one of the upper levels.

"Almost done," Emily said, grunting. "There!" She stood up and listened. "Coming this way. One more thing to do." She took out a little electronic device the size of a cell phone, punched a red button and pinged the locator. "Perfect. Let's go!" She picked up the flashlight and the empty epoxy tubes and they started for the stairwell just as lights swung down the ramp from the upper level.

"What did you come up with, Durwood?" There was more static than ever over the vid-phone. Naturally, the screen was blocked so he couldn't see him—a stock cheapo flag video had been inserted instead.

"I can't decide whether the assessments are true or not. He's definitely a weirdo though."

"I can see you're learning fast, Bob," Tercel whined. "Never give a straight answer unless you have to. Never show your cards. Maybe you'll go far, maybe you won't. I play it different though. I think you need all the friends you can get. ... I'm sending you some packages over. The stuff I mentioned about his friends and acquaintances. You probably heard I'm going to be gone for awhile."

"No," Bob admitted.

"A goodwill tour of Outer Mongolia. We're going to see if we can use it for some nuclear dumping. Could work out nice. Help their economy a lot. Help us out. I'll be gone for a while. Look the stuff over. I'd like to work together on this if we could. Pool our resources. Help each other out. Anyway, think it over." He hung up.

Bob yawned. Yeah, he would think it over, all right. He knew exactly what Tercel had in mind. He would do all the work, come up with the ideas and Tercel would step in and take all the credit. You didn't get as far up the ladder as

Tercel was without being shrewd and ruthless. He probably did need all the friends he could get—especially when it was time to look for someone else to step on.

Rammer

The monster rig had six wheels, each one over eight feet in diameter, with huge, cruel cleats. On the front, a large v-shaped blade protruded menacingly in front of the engine housing. The machine, painted a bilious yellow, was powered by a 1850 horsepower turbo-diesel engine.

Corvetta looked up at the huge beast in awe as Emily walked around it pointing out its various features.

"This is my baby," Emily said, patting one of the front tires. "Enough muscle here to blast anything off the road. Totally unstoppable. I could drive this right through a building if I wanted to."

Corvetta blinked in amazement. "I've seen these on the road, but I've never been up close to one before. It's so huge! It must be hard to drive. How do you do it?"

"It's not hard at all. It's easy in fact. It's got power everything. It can even be driven by remote control with a joy stick if you want to."

"I'd be afraid to death," said Corvetta, poking her head inside the dark archway of the oversized wheel well.

She leaned against the massive wheel and looked up

past the huge shock absorbers. "Oh, oh. What's that?... It looks like... Like..."

"Like what?" Emily said, frowning.

"Like someone is stuck up in there..."

"Let me see."

"Like a body or something... yuk!"

Emily pulled her aside, stuck her head in the opening, looked up along the shock absorber strut and said, "Damn!... You're right... I wonder how that bastard got there."

"Looks like some kind of Hispanic guy."

'I don't remember hitting any Hispanic assholes," Emily said, rubbing her chin with her fist.

"How about some Vietnamese guy? They look a lot alike at night."

"Nope."

"What should we do now?"

"Looks like he's wedged in there pretty good. What a pisser this is."

"Do you think we should try to get him out?"

"Nah! Not right now. Maybe he'll just fall out somewhere along the road. If not, I'll have to write up some kind of report. Those bastards in maintenance bitch like hell when they find bodies clogging up the machinery."

Corvetta took another peek inside. "He's right next to that big motor. Won't he start to smell when we're riding around?"

"Yeah, probably. But that won't be any problem for us. This thing has got a self-contained atmosphere that protects it even against poison gas attacks."

"Well, that's something anyway. I just hate unpleasant odors."

"What I can't figure out is where I nailed this guy. I hope he hasn't fucked up the steering."

"Maybe you were texting."

"Maybe . . . Oh, well." Emily took a set of keys out of her assault vest. She pointed the fob at the cabin and pushed the red button. Lights came on in the cockpit. At the same time the door slid open and a set of stairs folded out and descended to within a foot of the ground. It was like some kind of alien space ship. Emily reached a gloved hand over to Corvetta, pinched her on the cheek and winked. "Let's go hunting, princess!"

They went up the stairs, climbed into the cockpit and strapped themselves in. The stairs retracted and folded away. At Emily's loving touch, the huge machine suddenly came to life with a monstrous roar and a belch of black smoke.

Hunting Big Bob

The big wipers pulsed slowly and made a hissing sound in the gritty rain. They were idling on the shoulder at mile marker 78 just south of the Brookville overpass. Nearly two stories above the roadway, the huge yellow vehicle gave them an excellent view of the crawling lines of traffic. Emily had blasted one dead duck off the roadway already, and the driver had barely bailed out in time before she hit it. Corvetta squealed with delight when it disintegrated and was blown into the median. "Totally cool!" she said, admiring Emily's skill with the big rig.

"What time is it?" Emily asked.

Corvetta glanced at the instrument panel. "Five-forty."

"Good. We should be able to pick him up now." Emily punched in a series of numbers on the locator keypad, then hit enter. The screen went blank for a few seconds then came back with a map and a tiny dot of red against the background. "There he is," she said. She zoomed the screen fifty percent. "Twelve and a half miles north, right lane. Speed thirty-three miles per hour. Should be here in about twenty minutes if things don't slow." She looked over at Corvetta. "You ready for this, girl?"

Moving Target

The traffic inched by. Emily played with the adjustment levers on the big blade, fine tuning the angle and the height. "I want to hit the bastard just right. Window level I think. It doesn't give you the high pop-ups like a lower angle shot, but it's nearly always fatal."

"So we won't get to see him fly?"

"Probably not. It'll be more like a spray of parts. Depends a lot on the angle I hit him, and the impact velocity."

"I kind of wanted to see Bob flying through the air in that little shit car."

"Don't worry. It will still be pretty cool."

"I wonder if I'm going to miss him at all."

"What'd you mean?"

"Well, he did have some good points."

Emily made a face. "Yeah, right."

"He was ambitious."

"He was an ass-kisser."

"He always wanted to make something out of himself."

"Wanted to make it all right. Make it with other women! You *know* he's been fooling around. One of them horny little government bitches, banging her like a broken screen door in a Kansas tornado."

Corvetta smiled and looked out at the lines of creeping gray cars. "Well, this should cure him of that."

Emily winked and patted her on the knee. "This is where we stick it to him," she said. "Oh, oh. He's almost here." She pointed at the locator screen. "Two minutes. First thing we have to do is separate him from the pack. So I can get a good shot at him. Kind of like sheep dogs used to do back in the old days. Buckle up, babe. Here we go!"

The big engine roared. The massive cleated tires began to move and smoke began to pour out of the twin exhaust stacks. The huge rammer began to roll.

Bob left the office a half hour early. His attaché case was filled with notes and parts of files from the box El Supremo had given him. He had an angle he was working on but wanted to think about it a little more before bouncing it off Morganfliess. He felt like seeing her rather than going home, but resisted the idea and punched in the usual coordinates.

The weather was brown and dripping again. His little plastic car seemed slower, sadder and more confining than ever. Somehow things didn't seem so bleak when he was with Heidi. She had a way of lighting up the world for him with her quick foxy smile and go-to-hell attitude.

The ride home seemed longer and more tedious than ever. There had been a noticeable slowdown in the last few months. Traffic control was getting more and more erratic. The computers were starting to log people off at the wrong exits, sending them on long pointless side trips, rejecting their passwords, keeping them from logging off when they needed to. Dead units along the road were becoming commonplace. You now often saw people walking along the shoulder of the highway, their cheap little Asian cars abandoned in the distance. The rammers were kept busy, smacking them off the road as soon as they died. A typical trip home now saw at least two sailing in the air. Once a car died you were required by law to get out in a hurry. The rammers weren't required to check for occupants in non-moving vehicles. Their job was to keep traffic moving at all costs.

Something was going on just ahead. There was a big slowdown. Pulsing red lights throbbed in the gauzy atmosphere, casting an intermittent red glow over the moving herd of cars in front of him. He knew a rammer was at work somewhere up there. He scanned the com-links dial, hoping to pick up a local report. Flashes were coming in from all up and down the interstate. Numerous accidents and stoppages had snarled traffic.

The pack of autos lurched forward, stopping and starting in the gloomy haze. His windshield wipers clacked noisily. They sounded like they were about to go out. Pieces of debris and twisted car parts came into view on the muddy shoulders. A seat, a crushed steering wheel, part of a dashboard. There was a deafening blast of air horns—three shorts and a long. It was the signal a rammer was about engage a target. Flashing red lights turned in to a solid streak above the wall of vehicles. There was a loud metallic boom and he saw a spray of plastic and metal fragments above the roofs of the cars ahead.

"Someone got smacked good," Bob said, talking to himself. They crept forward a couple hundred yards and then finally began to pick up a little speed. He could see the angular tail end of the massive yellow rammer off to the side. The remains of its victim, a twisted pile of unidentifiable parts, lay smoking in front of the rammer's huge blade. "Hate to get hit by that bastard."

The rammer belched smoke. Its blade moved a few

ticks, like clicking teeth. The traffic lurched and crawled through the chemical laden mists. Bob looked out occasionally at the huge mega condos lining the road. How many people lived in those giant slabs of concrete he wondered. What did they all do in those boxes? "Oh, well, life on our planet. It's all good," he said softly.

A siren shattered the air behind him. Flashing lights appeared in his rear view mirror. A rammer in full attack mode was approaching him from behind, and accelerating rapidly. There was only one car between him and the charging machine.

Not So Fast

Emily did a victory lap around the motor pool. The vast yard, where rows of metal hanger-like buildings stood, was surrounded by a ten-foot chain link fence. Hundreds of rammers and pieces of rammers in various states of repair were parked in the rain. "This will call for a little celebration tonight," she said, pulling up to one of the bays.

Corvetta was shaking her head. "It all happened so fast. I can't believe it."

"When the *Emily* hits you, it's lights out, baby!" She pressed a green button on the dash and the large two-story metal door began to rattle open. "Now let's get this sled checked in." She eased the big rig into the gloomy diesel fumed interior, set the brake, turned off the huge motor, then the cockpit switches one by one.

Mbele Goodwin, the Nigerian crew chief for her machine, was standing by the foot of the ladder wearing a greasy orange baseball cap and sneakers. She gave him a thumbs-up as she climbed out of the cab.

He said, "How many today, bitch?" grinning up at her.

She smiled, cracked her gum, held up four fingers as she hopped to the floor in her paratrooper boots.

He laughed, and swung his head from side to side. "Damn! You one dangerous bitch."

She punched him on the arm. "You say the sweetest things, you old wanker." She pulled him aside by one of the work benches and said in a low voice, "Ah, look, Mbele ... I think I may have a little problem here."

He stared at her for a second, then rolled his big eyes. "Don't tell me. Let me guess. You got another toe jam."

"I'm not sure."

"Let's see," he said without enthusiasm. "Where is it?"

"Right front."

He grabbed a large drop light from the workbench, plugged it in, and went over to the wheel well. He put his head inside and eyeballed the interior. After a minute he pulled back out and shrugged. "Nothing here." He checked again to make sure, "Nope. ... Not a thing."

Emily looked relieved. "Must have dropped out along the road somewhere."

He switched the light off. "Nothing but hamburger by now. Well, that's good news anyways. I hate digging those nasty things out. All that gooey mess!"

She handed him the keys. "The paperwork is what

gets me."

On their way back home Emily and Corvetta stopped at a convenience store to pick up some snacks for Bob's bon voyage party. A dingy yellowish rain swept the streets and the parking lot, and steamed the windows. The world had the look of a dirty aquarium.

It was eight-thirty by the time they got back to the condo and parked Emily's Focke-Wulf on the first sub-level next to the elevator.

Corvetta said, "How do you rate getting a spot like this? We're down on the ninth level."

Emily peeled off her black driving gloves and smiled innocently. "The previous occupant had a small accident."

Corvetta stared at her for a long time, then said, "You're unbelievable."

Emily reached under the seat. "Check this out. I've got a bottle of genuine mescal. I figured something with a worm in it would be appropriate now that old Bob is missing in action."

"I've never had mescal."

"Good, we'll go up to your place and celebrate while we wait for the news that your poor dear hubby has met with a terrible accident."

"I know, we can burn his pictures one at a time."

The lights in the elevator were still broken. Fred, the security guard, was still at the front desk. He was wearing the same uniform, the same grumpy expression and had the same grimy clipboard. Everything was just the same. Yet today. she thought, the world had changed forever.

They got off the elevator on Corvetta's floor. No one

else was in the hallway. It seemed strange to Corvetta that for a building with so many residents the halls always seemed empty, as if no one was living here at all.

Emily said, "How much insurance did you have on the little fucker?"

"I don't know exactly. There's at least two policies on him. The government spares no expense to take care of themselves, even if they screw everybody else."

"You should go out tomorrow and buy something really nice."

Corvetta opened the door, let Emily go in ahead of her. "I've got just the thing—"

They both froze in their tracks.

"Hi, guys," Bob said. "What's up, some kind of party?"

They stared at him in open-mouthed horror—as though confronting some terrible fiend sent from hell.

"You guys must be mind readers," he said cheerily, looking all too real, and depressingly healthy. "I was just thinking about a little party myself." He took the bulging bags of snacks from their frozen fingers and transported it all to the kitchen. They could hear him banging around in there happily, saying something about a close call.

Emily gave Corvetta a thin-lipped icy look, then raised her eyes to the ceiling and said, "I think we are missing another tenant. The one that parks next to Bob. The one that drove a car you were *sure* was Bob's."

Corvetta blinked a few times, looking at herself in one of the mirrors. She formed her mouth into a tiny cute red circle, and said, "Oops!"

Red Alert

The warning bells went off at four in the morning. He didn't even have to get dressed since he was still working, sweating over the last minute details of his plan. He grabbed a few papers, rushed out of the house and punched in the coordinates, trying to control his excitement as the little car ground into gear and doggedly traced its way to the White House Situation Room.

The pieces had all fallen into place at once. There seemed to be a certain inevitability about it that appealed to Bob's sense of destiny. He was at the right spot at the right time with the right tools. It all fit like fate. What he had to do now was make sure the people around him didn't fuck up.

Programming the computers to search the air exhaust monitors was no problem once the right formulas were known and plugged in. Getting it all on-line was something else. But El Supremo had backed him up all the way—personally rolling into the National Computer Center, screaming and kicking ass, firing five people who looked incompetent and two who actually were.

He started with the batches of addresses Tercel had given—all of Quattlebaum's friends, relatives and acquaintances, no matter how distant—and worked out from there, neighborhood by neighborhood, city by city. At peak output it would be nothing less than a super-computerized bloodhound sniffing at Quattlebaum's heels twenty-four hours a day. Finding anything at the locations Tercel had provided seemed like a long shot, and he had resigned himself at the outset to a tedious and painstaking search. Luck was with him however, it had been less than a week when the alarms went off. Sweeter yet, Tercel was still blundering. around somewhere in Outer Mongolia. It would be much tougher for him to jump in and take the credit now.

"I hope it's not a false alarm," he said, pounding the steering wheel impatiently.

The car's computer said, "Your washer fluid is low."

He gave the console a vicious shot with his foot. "Can't we go any faster, you piece of crap?"

The car remained silent until they hit another bump in the road. It hiccupped and said, "Your mother is lonely."

—————————— **Sneak Previews** ——————————

Security checked his ID and retinal image for the fifth time and hurried him past the heavily armed human drones straight to the elevated command console. The blast-proof Situation Room in the basement of the Off-White house was nearly as big as a football field. Hundreds of huge view screens covered every inch of the reinforced concrete walls. The room bustled with military brass and smart, colorful uniforms he didn't recognize, probably some super secret intelligence wing. There was a hum of purposeful activity, muffled but intense conversations.

"Here he is, General," someone said as he bounded up the metal stairs. General Murkington, tall and barrel-chested, was in charge of military operations.

"What's the status, General? Can we confirm the readings yet?"

"Two visuals, so far," Murkington said.

"Not enough."

"They're good quality though. Colonel Wiggins, punch it up for him. Just check these out."

"Tell me what's happening first."

"The screen on the left. Live from the scene. A large block of condos in New Detroit. Three separate alarms. The unit on the building on the near corner, two interior units."

"Can it be an equipment malfunction?"

"The tech people say no. Less than one in twenty five hundred."

"Here's the video on the console. Mr. Quattlebaum himself."

"Looks pretty blurry to me."

"Human eyes don't mean a thing. It's the computer verification that counts. Optical recognition software says it's a dead on match."

Bob watched in fascination as the deployment of troops and weapons took place on the multiple screens. A triple ring of steel was quickly being thrown around the whole block. Helicopter gunships, tanks, artillery, specially trained commando units were sealing every possible means of escape.

"In five minutes a gnat won't be able to get out of there,"

Murkington said.

"One more confirmation and we call El Supremo."

"I already took the liberty," Murkington said.

Bob didn't like that idea, not playing by the book, but he didn't have time to complain. The stainless steel doors suddenly clanged open and El Supremo came rolling in on his turbocharged bed and a wave of Secret Service attendants.

————— Revenge Of The Couch Potatoes —————

"What in hell is going on?" El Supremo roared. The attendants were busting ass hauling El Supremo's bed up the narrow metal stairs to the elevated catwalk. A few cabinet members and assorted flunkies scrambled after them. "Is this it, or what? Gimme an update."

"Two visual confirmations, sir," General Murkington said, smoothly stepping in front of Bob. "We're expecting further reports any second."

"What about it, Bob? What do you say?"

Bob cleared his throat. "Looks good so far, sir. But we need more than two."

"How many? I don't want any mistakes. I want to be dead certain."

"Launch protocol requires at least four grade ten confirmations."

"Grade ten all the way," Murkington said. "Let me show you. Colonel Wiggins, punch it up on the console again."

Colonel Wiggins bent over and stabbed at the keyboard. Quattlebaum's blurry outline jumped to the screen again.

"Computer enhancement confirms—"

"Never mind computer enhancement," El Supremo said, his face twisting with hatred. "That's him all right. I'd recognize that mug anywhere."

A female captain with red hair suddenly appeared at Murkinton's side and handed him a tabbed plastic folder. Murkington studied it a minute, then said, "Sir, another confirmed from Section Five." He inserted the disk himself and punched it up. "Here it comes now."

It was Quattlebaum in different light—an interior hallway seen from above. He was carrying a large bird on his shoulder. You could even read the pizza box.

"The ghost materializes," El Supremo said, hypnotized, his voice barely a whisper.

"Confidence level ten plus, sir."

"Deployment status, Murkington?"

"Proceeding at Full Emergency. We'll be able to launch all options in ... Wiggins?"

Colonel Wiggins looked at his watch. "Fourteen minutes, Twelve seconds, sir."

El Supremo nodded, then permitted himself a smile, "Good."

The five Secret Service men were all nodding too.

The fourteen minutes seemed like an eternity, every second multiplied hundreds of times on hundreds of different screens, each showing a different view of the operation—troops and equipment moving, aircraft taking off, helicopters orbiting in position, officers barking orders.

"Thirty seconds," someone said finally. Murkington turned to El Supremo. "Everything checks, sir. On your command."

El Supremo gave the nod and the assault began.

First came the softening up with heavy artillery. The initial barrage seemed to raise the whole block off the ground for a shocked instant before it began to settle back, then submerge in a sea of smoke and flames. A few seconds later the Strategic Air Command payloads began arriving, adding some powerful bass notes to the shrill of artillery. Smoke was everywhere now and beginning to obscure the cameras, giving the scene an eerie twilight cast.

"Can't we get any better video than this?" El Supremo complained.

"Too dangerous, sir. If the camera ships go any closer they could get hit themselves."

"Dammit, I want pictures! Tell them to go in closer."

Murkington spun on his heel, turning to Wiggins. "Tell them to get closer."

"Yes, sir."

Flames and destruction filled all the screens. Devastation on all channels. Miraculously, pieces of the building were still standing amid towering columns of fire.

"Now this is more like it," El Supremo said as the camera ships went in tighter.

The contents of a balcony came into view. A coffee table and some plastic chairs were beginning to melt and ooze towards the edge.

"Look, you can actually see some poor bastard." A different angle showed a figure staggering from the sliding glass door to the railing. He was covered with soot, gesturing furiously towards the cameras. "Zoom in on this guy. He looks familiar."

"Quattlebaum?" someone asked.

"No, too fat. Way too fat. ... Looks familiar though."

They lost him for a second behind a curtain of smoke. Then he reappeared, larger, more frightening. He was shaking his fist and gasping for air. His eyes rolled wildly in his head.

"Holy shit! It's Senator Krenmeister!" Murkington announced in disbelief.

"You're right. It is Krenmeister. I'd recognize that fat slob anywhere."

"Sir, should we call it off?"

Krenmeister seemed to be looking straight at them now, his eyes wide with terror, his thick jowls flapping soundlessly.

"Dammit, what's that stupid bastard doing there?" El Supremo said.

"He was scheduled to visit some of his constituents

this week, sir," Colonel Wiggins put in helpfully. "Go to an old folks home, I believe. New Detroit is his district."

"Quattlebaum would have to pick the same damn block for his pizza treat."

"Shall we call it off, sir?"

"Call it off?" El Supremo said angrily, rotating on his bed.

"It will look awful bad, sir."

Murkington elbowed Wiggins aside. "Sir, we're still getting positive readouts on Quattlebaum's position. We need to launch Phase Two within ten seconds or we could lose him."

El Supremo turned to Milton Klopman, the Secretary of State. "How bad?"

"Very bad, sir." Klopman said, shaking his head. Klopman was one of the few members of the Inner Circle still ambulatory. He did have two metal legs and a glass eye, however.

The camera moved in closer to Krenmeister who had run to the other side of the balcony. His hair appeared to be smoking. He looked like he was shouting or praying.

"You're right. It will be very bad. Besides, he's the heart and soul of all the legislation I've been getting through. I've relied on his judgment for years. There's only one thing we can do ... Murkington..."

"Sir?"

"Blow the idiot away! Launch every damn thing you can get your hands on. Use the blockbuster. I want to make sure Quattlebaum is dead once and for all."

Murkington saluted sharply. "Yes, sir." He turned on

his heel to give the order himself. The blockbuster was one of his favorites—it packed the power of a small nuclear weapon but left none of the troublesome radiation. It was a totally safe weapon environmentally.

"We'll just have to put the lid down hard on this one," El Supremo was explaining. "A giant meteorite maybe. ....Androids from Pluto. Blame it on any goddam thing. I want the whole area quarantined. No press. No talk show hosts. None of those morons at CNN. Nobody that I don't hand pick. We'll just have to tough it out."

Klopman pulled a face. "I don't know. It's a big load to swallow."

El Supremo cranked the bed in a slow circle so he could face Klopman. He said through clenched teeth, "I am the President of the United States of America. You don't get to be President without being the best damn salesman in the country. We'll make them eat it!"

The light struck Bob's face at an odd angle, streaming in from the top of the mullioned widows straight into his eyes. He blinked groggily and looked around the room. He would have to get used to it: the light, the room, with its heavy wood paneling and expensive masses of furniture. He smiled and tried to concentrate. Someone was talking, explaining something in measured, confident tones just a few feet from where he was. He suddenly remembered they were talking about him and twisted his head around to get a better look.

El Supremo was looking straight at him, grinning, his head as big as a Buddha in the flinty sunlight. Bob felt a sudden, sharp pang of gratitude and pride as he blinked and tried to collect his thoughts. He would have to say something soon, express his gratitude for the honor they had bestowed upon him.

"The only true judge of a man is by the loyalty he shows to his friends." El Supremo said. "The rest is all bullshit. Welcome to the club, Bob."

There were some groans of assent and then a lot of slurping as they all sipped whiskey through their straws. The faces all seemed slightly warped, as though seen through the sides of a specimen bottle, gray, indistinct, their features imperfectly formed. Yet they were the faces of power, and each one was at the center of a web of relations that exercised nearly absolute control over the government, the very life of everyone in the country. And Bob was now part of that select group: The Inner Circle.

He would get used to the strangeness of it all. The bed, the light at odd angles, the difference in perspectives, the inability to use his arms and legs. These would pass the doctors assured him, as swiftly as the discomfort of the operation. The drugs would keep him in a state of euphoria while he acclimated to having others do the mundane chores he used to have to do himself. His wishes would now be someone's patriotic duty to perform, his slightest whim would be attended to instantly by a well paid staff of nurses and minor government functionaries. Yes, he would get used to the odd perspectives, the deference of subordinates as they rolled him around the halls of power. . . .

And then there was always Corvetta. She had never been so passionate as when she realized that though physically he was a vegetable, socially and politically he was a superstar. His new lifestyle was working out just fine he decided, mumbling vaguely. He was still slightly dazed and stumbled through the formalities as best he could, thanking his new colleagues for their support and what a high honor it was to join their august ranks and similar kinds of bullshit. They all drank some more whiskey, congratulated themselves again, and then suddenly it was all over and the pushers began wheeling them out one at a time.

"Damn fine job, Bob," he remembers El Supremo saying, winking slyly as his Secret Service pusher rolls him past the huge, gleaming desk.

Bob nods back and is suddenly in the hall and part of a weird autocade as the Inner Circle splits up into its various destinations. He allows himself a luxurious sigh and replays in his mind's eye the conspiratorial wink El Supremo gave him. A true insider's wink now. Success really is opportunity meeting preparation, he decided. As corny as it sounded, the old saying was true, and in is heart he was glad he was an American.

—— Recollections Of The Golden Triangle ——

"Before our little criminal enterprise you said if I helped you it would all come full circle."

"It has in a sense. But there are always circles within circles, puzzles within puzzles. You've got all the pieces. The Q file was the key piece."

"I don't see it. I don't see any circles. Just little dots that don't connect. My focus was originally on Mote to see if he was some kind of plant or had gone rogue. He had no relation to the Q file."

"That's where you're wrong, my boy. He was involved with the file just after it disappeared. And so were you."

"Me?"

"Certainly. The Zipsky imbroglio. Remember?"

L. looked at him incredulously. "What the hell does Zipsky have to do with this. That's ancient history."

"Your assignment to investigate Mote, then Bob

Durwood, then his girlfriend. And, of course recovering the file. You weren't the only one tasked with that assignment by the way. Dozens of agents were."

"But Zipsky was old news. It happened before I even joined the agency."

"Zipsky was killed for that file. He didn't even know what it was when he stole it from the deep cover Israeli agent he was working for as a chauffeur. The guy went in to take a piss at a gas station and Zipsky lifted it out of his briefcase along with some working cash."

"How did the Israelis get it?"

"Stole it from the guys who assembled it. If you remember, they all disappeared under rather suspicious circumstances."

"But why would they want it? They're our allies."

"Right. They're our big friends. They just wanted to insure we stay their big friends. They knew there were people in the State Department who were getting weary of them controlling our foreign policy in the Middle East. They wanted a little extra insurance. It was important enough to take out Zipsky to get it back."

"But why a bomb? That seems a little too high profile."

"The one his mother sent didn't actually work. They helped her out by sending a second one. One that did. They had to move fast, before you and Mote got there."

"But the burned piece of letter with her name on it?"

"Israeli intelligence again. They knew from an employee at the retirement home that she hated him, had ordered some worthless junk to make a bomb."

"So they framed his mother?"

"They just helped her own plan along. They did pay for that idiot lawyer she had. They were convinced he would actually get her off."

"The FBI never let on there was a file involved. Even the case file now makes no mention of it."

"The FBI didn't want it to come to light either. They buried part of it. You saw the sanitized version. Israel has a strong lobby. Both inside and outside the government. They just wanted to make sure everything looked neat and clean from their point of view."

"In a way it's too bad Durwood never got his hands on the file. Might have changed his mind. Things might have turned out differently if he had."

"I doubt it. Durwood is an all too common type: too devoted to someone else's idea of success to see where his best interests lie. He gave up Morganfliess to take another step up the ladder."

"And my old friend Mote?"

"Mote, though he still doesn't know it, was co-opted by a cabal within the agency. There are several groups vying for power that could have misappropriated him. He's loyal, unquestioning, obviously a pawn for someone, and can easily be hung out to dry. A most useful man. The world depends on people like Mote. Governments couldn't run without them. He'll retire to Florida one day, watch the oil spills wash to shore, the sand turn from gray to black and wonder ... what?"

There is still some uncertainty in Bob's history, beginning as he rolled down the hall towards the VIP exit. Perhaps it was at one of the checkpoints inside, or in the sheltered portico as he waited for transportation. There was a mix-up there. The Secretary of State's car had been delivered by mistake and he had to wait while they sorted things out. Then there was the mysterious call. He was paged to one of the waiting areas, but when he got there no one showed, and there was confusion. The switch could have happened at any one of these places.

He was still intoxicated from the medication, from El Supremo's whiskey and attention. The next thing he remembers with any clarity was the horizon lurching and the clatter of wheels on asphalt as he was rolled across the parking lot. It seemed strange that no one else was in sight, none of his peers. "Where am I ?" he said impatiently, suddenly feeling more like a load of groceries than a key member of the government.

An open hand appeared over Bob's face. It hung there for a second then pinched him on the nose. "Wake up, Bob, we're going for a ride!"

Bob was shocked, outraged by the impertinence. "What do you think you're doing?" he blubbered.

"That's it, Bob, try to stay awake." the voice encouraged. Bob was, in fact, beginning to shake off his mental torpor, a process that was speeded up dramatically when he noted with some alarm his attendant was attaching his bed to the back of an automobile with some bunge cords.

"What are you doing?" His voice was a little panicky now.

"Gotta wear this, Bob." The man jammed a red crash helmet on his head. "Never know what we might run into. We better tighten these straps, too. Wouldn't want you flying off when we reach warp speed."

"You're not my attendant," Bob yelped, cranking his neck around, trying to get a better look at the man. "Who are you anyway?"

The door closed, biting off Bob's question. The engine that started was deep throated and powerful sounding. The last of Bob's cobwebs were gone by the time they reached the Washington monument going fifty.

"Gotta hand it to those Lay-Z-Dude beds, Bob. Those babies have pretty good wheels." The crash helmet had a built in mike and headset. Bob was fully conscious by this time, alert, and screaming at the top of his lungs.

"Can't make out what you're saying, Bob. You're breaking up a little. Don't worry though, we'll pick up some real speed when we hit the expressway. I had all the governors unplugged so this thing can really fly."

Bob's momentary spell of clarity, brought on by a sudden rush of adrenaline, was quickly replaced by a fog of blind terror. No one could say with any certainty when the first wheel, squealing and smoking, exploded off the bed, since it was never found. They were well beyond the 100 mph mark according to some monitoring devices, that much was certain anyway.

"You're lookin' good back there, Bob. Just try to keep your weight a little more centered."

Bob radioed back a series of screams.

"Didn't quite catch that, Bob... Anyway, the hardest part was finding a decent pizza ... Beer wasn't that easy either, come to think of it. Too many anti-drinking zealots around. Getting the army to blow up Krenmeister's condo was a fairly interesting challenge intellectually. You've probably guessed that I impersonated Tercel on the phone, and Burdley of course ..."

——————— **Cut!** ———————

"I don't know if I can do this?"

"Why not?

"I don't know where it's going."

"You're supposed to be a film editor."

"But it makes no sense. There's no story, no plot."

"Didn't you look at the script?"

"That's what I mean. At first I thought it was just a bunch of gibberish. Then I realized it was not even that good."

"You're thinking about this all wrong. You're trying to fit everything in a nice neat box. Plot, character, dialog, blah, blah, blah. Try to be more artistic."

"Okay, I still don't know where it's going. It doesn't

make any sense."

"Movies don't have to make any sense. They just have to make money."

"Look, we've got all these dailies here but I can't recognize any discernible pattern. What's this turkey supposed to be, a thriller, a comedy, a tragi-comedy, a historical-comical-tragedy?"

"Okay, okay! I'll give you some help here."

"Well . . .?"

"I'm thinking."

"I think you're wasting your time. It's hopeless. We ought to just trash it."

"We can't. We got big bucks in it already. Just think of it as a parable."

"A parable? This stew of inanities?"

"Absolutely. Unfettered ambition, the lust for power in a society gone mad, a culture gone haywire."

"Are we looking at the same footage? What's this government agent got to do with it? What's he doing sneaking around going to Beirut?"

"I dunno. I dropped the shooting script and it got mixed up with a bunch of papers some guy gave me at a Mexican restaurant. Everyone's got a screenplay these days."

"Why did I get into this business in the first place?"

"You worry too much. Movies haven't made sense for years. Coherent plots are a thing of the past. You don't need them any more."

"I don't know. It just doesn't seem right somehow. Maybe I'm out of touch. I can't help thinking that after all this work it should make some sense."

"Look at it this way, pal. Life doesn't make any sense. It's like a bad movie too. So why let it bother you?"

The Big Enchilada

The bed was only occasionally touching the roadway now, bouncing and wobbling violently in a series of erratic hops. Bob could see the wide-eyed startled look on the faces of other motorists as they careened past.

"I'm still surprised no one has figured it out yet ... Anyway, after I broke into the computers I simply changed the grid coordinates by two blocks. When you saw me entering the hallway with the pizza I was actually two blocks south of the readouts you were getting ... Poor old Krenmeister ... Oh well, not a bad way to go when you think about it. A true American hero, battling tooth and nail on the patio of his condo, fighting to the last."

The bed was completely off the ground, planing and twisting like the tail of a kite over the back of the powerful little truck.

Then the bunge cords went, sending Bob rocketing off the exit ramp, across a service station parking lot, through the lube racks and out the other side and into the prickly pear shrubbery of a Taco Matic restaurant. Had the cords simply snapped, or were they purposely released? Again something of a mystery that Bob wasn't much help resolving, being totally preoccupied at the time with keeping his center of gravity low and some highly creative howling. Dave, the assistant manager, and Louie the fry cook, who had watched Bob's trajectory in awe and amazement, both rushed outside when he hit and tried to see under all the broken cactus.

"Man that's gotta smart," Louie the fry cook said, wincing and shaking his head.

"Geez, what a mess!"

"What's he saying, anyway?"

"Mumbling something about a big enchilada."

"We better not take any chances with him."

"You're right" Dave said. "Better give him the Mega Burro and Super Enchilada Combo."

"Gotcha. … What about something to drink?"

"I'll ask him."

Bob was a little vague on the drinks, now apparently more interested in perfecting some poultry noises.

"That'll be twenty-two fifty."

Bob's eyes were just visible behind the cactus pads, darting around like pinballs. "Cluck, cluck," he responded.

"I said twenty-two fifty, dude." Dave was waving a bag of food at him now, trying to get his attention.

Things might have turned out differently for Bob and his tenuous grip on sanity if fate hadn't suddenly taken over here in the form of Conrad Mote who came squealing into the parking lot on two flat tires, bouncing over the curbs and speed bumps. He screeched to a halt and was out of the car in an instant.

"Bob? Dammit, I knew that was you," he said, pushing the assistant manager out of the way. "Stand back, meatball! Official business. ... Here, let me help you out of there."

"This guy owes me twenty-two fifty."

"Didn't I tell you to buzz off," Mote warned.

"But he owes me—"

Mote took his pistol out and fired a couple warning shots through the plate glass window, causing the assistant manager and fry cook to disappear in a whirl of pumping arms and legs.

"I was going in the opposite direction when I see this thing flying down the median. It looks like a damn bed. The next thing I know it's coming straight for me. Then I see this big face go right by my window and I think, Holy Shit! That looks like Bob."

"Yup, yup... the big enchilada," Bob was saying, his eyes were still making fast orbits inside his skull.

"No time to eat now, pal. Here, let me help you in." He opened the door to his car and threw Bob on the front seat and jumped behind the wheel. "Anyway, I'm looking into the rearview mirror to see where you went when all the alarms and buzzers go off. Peruvian terrorists all over the place control says. So that's when I figure out what you're up to, tailing these guys. Leave it to old Bob to be right in the middle of all the action... What a coincidence, right? What was that, some kind of new motorized thing? "

Bob was dangling from the harness, looking around at the inside of Mote's vehicle as it began to move. His eyes grew wider and began to fill with terror as they began to lurch and bound, heedless of curbs or obstacles.

"Man, this is great, isn't it? Just like old times. Hang on, Bob, were starting to roll now. We'll catch those Panamanian bastards or die trying!"

They hit the highway and began to steadily accelerate in spite of the two flat tires.

=== **THE END** ===